This is My Story

Flairs and Glairs
Publication House

Disclaimer

This is a work of fiction and solely represent the thoughts of the corresponding authors of the articles. Our editors have tried their best to edit the content of all the authors and check the plagiarism.
All the write-ups in this book are unique and are only published in this book.
In case any plagiarism or error is found, only the author is responsible alone, and not the publisher or the Compilers.

Cover Designing and Book Formatting
Shubham Shah and Ishani Agarwal

Acknowledgement

I am thankful to God for giving me direction to express myself and find myself again in such a beautiful manner. I am thankful to my parents for such an amazing support and trust on me and my sister for always encouraging me.

I would like to extend my heartfelt gratitude towards all the co-authors who have been with me in this wonderful journey. I had their constant support and kindness, and this project would never have been possible without their co-operation and patience. Each and every co-author has put his/her best creative hand and language skill for this anthology. Thanks to all my co-authors for being such an amazing and cooperative with me during this journey.

I would also like to thank Flairs & Glairs Publication for giving this wonderful opportunity. Their constant guidance and encouragement towards us has given wings to this project's success.

Thankful gratitude towards all those who have worked hard and made an effort for his book to be successful.

Co Author

Shubham Shah (Founder Flairs And Glairs)
Ishani Agarwal (Co Founder Flairs And Glairs)
Compiler- Vaishnavi Hend

1. Vaibhav (Shikhar)
2. Kale Jayesh Arvind
3. Samir Gope
4. Vijay Lakshmi Yaduvanshi
5. Salman Mohammed
6. Abidul Haque
7. Ankit Topwal
8. Rishi Singh
9. Pavithra Mohanraj
10. Annawasha Naskar
11. Krishna Tangariya
12. Mrunal Hatwar
13. Dr Nirankush V Khubalkar
14. Chanchal Punyani
15. Nawab Azhar
16. Manoj Agarwal
17. Kaushal Manpreet
18. Atif Nawab
19. Aman Sharma
20. Sarvesh Kumar
21. Izhar
22. Srishti Rani Panda
23. Tannu Sahay
24. Apeksha
25. Karthik Karty
26. Priyanka Yadav
27. Navjot Singh
28. D A Blithe

29. Sujit Pawar
30. Payal Goswami
31. Ravina Thadani
32. Vaibhav Dev Singh
33. Dr. Pranoti Sakhare
34. Ankita Sharma
35. Jaz Gill
36. Imroz Raza
37. Robin Singh Rathore
38. Rudra Prasad
39. Raman Shant
40. Prayksha Pandit
41. Payal Indani
42. Dr. Shreeja Singh Chandel
43. Pooja Indani
44. Shweta Taikar
45. Ketan Nag (Neeket)
46. Pujitha Atyam
47. Namita Arora
48. Asrar ul Hassan
49. Ashita Sharma
50. Susmita Kar

Shubham Shah

(Founder- Flairs and Glairs)

Shubham Shah, an entrepreneur at "Flairs & Glairs" a brand with dynamics in events organizing and cultural educational pan INDIA, is a 26yrs old guy who recently has entered the digital platform of imprinting emotions. He has initiated with his own open mic platform to help budding poets and aspiring writers under his brand named as "Teekhe Zasbaaat"

He is a commerce graduate from the Bhagalpur City of Bihar. He states Writing has impersonated him since childhood and he has now been writing for over a decade!

Cooking, on the other hand, is his passion! He also mentions, trying out new things just tickles him!

When asked sir, Why SPICY EMOTIONS?

He smiled and added, "agar jasbaat teekhe na ho toh wo jasbaat kahan" Spices are all that blends! So do his words!

As a chef, he presents to you his dish! Hot and freshly served! Taste it! Feel it! Enjoy it! You can also find his writing in the Book "Teekhe Zasbaaat" and 50+ Co-authored anthologies. With his passion to explore opportunities across Platforms, he is working with keen devotion and We wish him all the very best for his future ventures.

He is Featured in the International Magazine DeMode for his upcoming solo novel.

He is Approved by Ne8x for its Lit Fest, and is a Golden Star Awards 2020 Winner.

He is a India Book of Records Holder for his Anthology Satrang, and has the Grandmaster title by Asia Book of Records, for the same.

He has also been featured in Prabhat Khabar, Dainik Jagran, and a lot of other Newspapers in Bihar for his achievements.

He has been a proud co-author to

India Book Of Records (Title- Black)

World Book Of Records (Title -15 Wonders of Poetries)

India Book Of Records (Title - Aaina)

Vajra World Records Holder (Title - Gustakhi Maaf Hai)

High Range of Records Holder (Title - Gustakhi Maaf Hai)

Indian Book of Records

(Title - Road from Worst to Best)

Share your reviews on his

INSTAGRAM

@spicy_emotions
@shubham4shah

Or via email on

shubham2shah@gmail.com

To stay tuned to his work and opportunities follow his business Handles

INSTAGRAM   FACEBOOK   YOUTUBE

@flairsandglairs
@teekhezasbaaat

WEBSITE:

https://flairsandglairs.in/
https://flairsandglairs.com/

Ishani Agarwal

(Co-Founder- Flairs and Glairs)

Ishani Agarwal hails from the City of Joy, Kolkata.

She is the co-founder of her Community "Teekhe Zasbaaat" and Flairs and Glairs Publication.

Been a Compiler for 45+ Anthologies, she is in the process for more. Co-authored in 150+ Anthologies. She is a India Book of Records Holder, a Vajra World Records Holder, a High Range of Records Holder, an OMG Book of Records Holder, a Bravo Record holder, a Forever Star Book of World Records and an Indian Book of Records Holder.

Approved by Ne8x for its Lit Fest 2020, and Literary Icon 2020. Also a Golden Star Awards Winner 2020.

She has also been awarded with India Star Republic Award 2021, a part of She Awards by Awards Arc and Winner of Nari Samman 2021 by Literoma.

She is also selected as Best Achiever of the Year by AwardsArc and Most Challenging Compiler Award by Spectrum Awards.
She got her first solo Published,a solo Compilation consisting of first 750 contents of hers, titled "Hand That Burnt While Healing".

She has been featured by the National Magazine "Taree Zameen Par" with the title 'unstoppable'.
Also featured in the International Magazine DeMode for her upcoming solo novel, she is proud to write on social issues, and is happy with the love she is receiving.
Connect with her on Instagram: @Ishani_agarwal_quotes / @compilations_so_far

Vaishnavi Hend
Compiler

An ardent writer, versifier and a poetess who writes her emotions and point of views while radiating in her own vibrations. "A person can easily give a right direction to his/her compressed voice, thoughts, emotions and desires by just choosing to pen down on paper" is what her view towards Writing. She started her writing journey as an amateur writer by her own choice. She is an author of a number of anthologies along with a world record anthology- "It's me in My Prime". She is also the compiler of "CHIMERA", "BLINK TO THINK", "VIBGYOR" and "P FOR PERFECT" anthologies. You can get to her by typing- Blink2Think-B2T on YouTube and blink2think_insta_official on Instagram.

This Is My Story

We all are having the significant quality of existence called
"LIFE"
But we all are having this life with lots of dissimilarities,
uncommonly rife
We all have untold things, memories, feelings, unsaid words
We often can't say it all because we are attached to some
invisible cords
Cords of fear, restrictions, suppressions, allegations, the list is
long
But why it matters to us, why we prove them right and prove
ourselves wrong?
We often live in depression, only one question again and again
we ask,
How long this pain will last and will my past ever stay in the
past?
No one understands, what you feel is what we feel
But the truth is always yours which no one can steal
What they feel about you, judge about you, say about you,
How does it really matters?
They were not there when it happened,
Then how do they call them our near ones, well-wishers or
advisors
Why this silence?
Nowadays people think silence is equal to an introvert
But tell them you also have a story, you are not a silent nerd
Giving a chance to yourself is a better appeal
Too many scars are there that you have to heal
Healing the pain and getting ready for the better future,
Isn't it the best deal?
So break this silence, but don't make noise
Tell them everything with your crystal clear voice

If everyone has a valuable life then why only celebrities have their biography?
Open up your heart, feel proud to be an ordinary
Tell them prominently,
This Is My Story.

Tell Me Your Story

Every time when I look in your eyes
I see you broken inside, trying to fight by your side
I just want to feel your feelings
That you can't say by your side
Things that you want always hide...
I want to see you,
Want to be with you,
And I want to hear you clearly…
So tell me your story, so tell me your sadness
I want u to keep my side and just look in your eyes
So tell me your story, I know that you're sorry
Oh please don't leave me now...you just hold my hand tight
And tell me your story.

Every feeling, every inch of you
All that I want to know you,
All that you don't like talk to
When I close my eyes,
I can't stop thinking of you
Even I try to…
I know that it hurt you, I know that it haunt you
You just believe me that, everything will be alright
So tell me your story tell me your sadness
I want you to keep my side and just look in your eyes
So tell me your story, I know that you're sorry
Oh please don't leave me now...you just hold my hand tight
Let's make a new story...

Vaibhav (Shikhar)

I have just sparked my pen into this writing world. Wanna tell and make people feel through my words and seeking for your love and blessings.
insta id- vaibhav_thoughts

A Fake Friend

'A friend in need
Is a friend in deed',
But the friend who was
Not the friend i need.

Being best with me
Was all i need,
But the face he shown
Was the fakest i seen.

Being true with me
Was all i expect,
But the way he betrayed
Was the gift i get.

He'll stand with me
Was the help i want,
But how he made me down
Made my heart haunt.

Don't you believe
How i got in trap,
World is full of mean
Don't regret and forget.

Kale Jayesh Arvind

My self Kale Jayesh Arvind I live in Nashik, Maharashtra.
Student of Ty BBA and acknowledge from Bharma Valley
College Nashik.
I'm happy and I don't think there is any big kind of an
achievement anybody can have.
I just love to write and love to play...

आसान नहीं होता है ।

किसीको चुन कर उससे इश्क करना
फिर उसकी ना पर ना सुन्न
कई दिनों तक उसके पीछे पड़ना
और उसके ना वाली नदानीयो को हा में बदलना
आसान नहीं होता है ।
एक नए रिश्ते की शुरुआत करना
किसीको पता ना चले ये खयाल रखना
छुप छुपके एक दुसरे को ताकना
और क्लास bunk करके उनसे मिलने जाना
आसान नाही होता है
फिर caste और religion वाली बातों का शुरू होना
एक दुसरे को खोने के डर से रोना
रात रात भर घब्राहट में सोना
और एक दिन इसी वजह से एक दुसरे को खोना
आसान नहीं होता है ।

एक तुही

खुशियो भरा प्यार हो
एक तुही मेरा यार हो
मै सारा जहा छोड दु
बस तेरा ही दिलदार हो
हम एक जान एक सास हो
एक दुसरे के लिये खास हो
मै मांगा कुछ खुदासे बस तुही मेरे पास हो
कुछ अनकही बाते अब हो
जो होना हे यो सब हो
मै मन्नते तुझ से करू
और तुही मेरा रब हो
तु हसे तो शाम हो
और प्यार भरा हो
शादी की छवि पर
तेरा मेरा नाम हो

Samir Gope

He is Samir Gope he live in Jamshedpur, Jharkhand. He is writer, co - author, photographer and also youtuber.

अकेला योद्धा

मैं अकेला योद्धा हूँ ।
मैं अकेला योद्धा हूँ ।
सफर मेरा है ,
हालात मेरा है ।
ना कोई मेरा दुख सहेगा ,
ना कोई मेरा सुख भोगेगा ।
एकांत रह कर खुद को परखा हूँ ।
एकांत रह कर खुद को जाना हूँ ।
मैं अकेला योद्धा हूँ ।
मैं अकेला योद्धा हूँ ।

ये

ये सफलता मेरे संघर्ष का है ,
कोई छीन नहीं सकता ।
ये रणनीति मेरे स्थिर मन का है ,
कोई बदल नहीं सकता ।

ये प्रेम मेरा दिल से है ,
कोई नफरत घोल नहीं सकता ।
ये पहचान मेरे खुद का है ,
कोई छिपा नहीं सकता ।

ये विश्वास मेरातुम पर है ,
कोई झुठला नहीं सकता ।
ये मेरे अटल इरादें हैं ,
कोई मिटा नहीं सकता ।

Vijay Lakshmi Yaduvanshi

Vijay Lakshmi Yaduvanshi, a budding writer from UP. She loves to write about childhood memories, parents love, self worth, friendship, love, betrayal, farmers etc. She started writing in the year 2018, basically write in Hindi and Hinglish. Instagram id: - Poetical_gril

Khud Ko Khojne Ki Chah

Nikal padi hu ek anjaani si raah me
Khud ko khojne ki chah me
Ek bar phir se khud ko khojne ki chah me
Na jaane ab ye safar kaisa hoga
Lmba hoga ya chota hoga
Aasan hoga ya mushkilo bhra hoga
Ek anjaana sa raah hoga
Jispe na koi mera humraah hoga
Ek bar phir nikal padi hu mai khud ko khojne ki chah me
Ek anjaani si raah me
Bs khud ko khojne ki chah me

Maa Ka Aanchal

Meri bs ek hi hai khwaish
Mai phir se bachpan me chali jau
Phir whi nanhi si bachchi bn jau
Maa k aanchal se phir se wo luka-chuppi ka khel- khel pau
Ek bar phir se uski anchal me chup jau
Duniya k har maslon se tanhaa ho jau
Apne sare drd-o-gm bhul phir se usse lipat jau
Kaash phir se mai bachpan me chali jau phir se maa ki o
nanhi si bachchi bn jau
Maa k aanchal se phir se khel-khel pau

Mohd Salman

Mohd Saalman from Medchal district Telangana.
as a final year student of MLR Institute of Technology in the stream of mechanical department. I Developed skills on manufacturing things and product designing.
Indian Engineering system has to deal with a lot of theory papers which is required to scramble students head luckily I found my happiness in writing and reading

Rusted Bars

-The rusted bars tells you the value of free life.

-It has heard many stories and had received many tattoos on the walls which holds the rusted bars.

-Even the flow of Tears can't be melted the rusted bars.

-At some point I get a doubt that are the rusted bars are deaf else my voice is weak.

-Hacksaw teeths are weaker than the rusted bars.

-they say Even the animal becomes a man behind it but a man becomes an animal behind the rusted bars.

-I had found that outside the rusted bar everyone had a different hope of dream but inside the rusted bar an single hope of dream for everyone.

Some count days like years some years like days.

-Many here has been experienced the Ray of hope comes and goes with Tears in a short span of time.

-even a child separates mother's womb after 9 months and when will I get separate from this womb.

-School kid office man leave the job at 5 p.m. but when will I leave from this place.

-My hope of ejecting the rusted bars are drowning after every hearing.

The NGOs can't swipe the pain from more hearts.

-My fingers slide over the bars and give the bgm to my painful sorrow.

-I get a Question to myself that why god does not listen to us does he punishes us this cruelly. I had received my punishment yet he doesn't listen to us.

I get a lump in my throat whenever my family stands after the rusted bars.

Abidul Haque

Abidul Haque
Engineer
Writer
Musician
Composer
I write lyrics, shayari and poem. I basically write in English and Hinglish. Love and sad poems and quotes. Heart touching and Real facts..
Instragram ID: - abidul_quotes haque_abidul

I'm Happy Once Again

Yes I'm changed
I'm no more the same
Not running behind u again
Ur attraction is no more attracting me
Yes I'm happy once again

I'm no more waiting for ur love
I'm no more waiting for ur text
U can see a bright smile on my face
Yes I'm happy once again

I'm no more wasting my time
I'm keeping ur love behind
Forgetting our memories aside
By creating a new one beside
Yes I'm happy once again......

Your Memories

Your memories are beautiful
Just like my old school
Cannot see or touch
But can feel so much.
Your memories are buried in my heart
Which cannot be dissolved
Just like the deep well
My heart has become a hell.
Your memories are not flying
Which keep me reminding
Love is not for everyone
Thatalways turned out to be unfaithful.
Your memories are not vanishing
From which I'm always hiding
That makes me cry
That makes me cry.

Ankit Topwal

Ankit Topwal is from Rishikesh, Uttarakhand. He is a college student with science stream. He loves to read stories like love, horror, heart touchable story etc. , And also like to write some different own lines...
Instagram id: - ankittopwal14

अकेला था अकेला रह गया

यहां अपने जीवन का जो किस्सा आप सभी को मैं बताने जा रहा हूं वो मेरे लिए अच्छा और बुरा दोनों अनुभव रहा है !

यह बात 2017 की है , उस समय मैं स्वयं को बहुत ही अकेला महसूस करता था , दोस्त तो थे लेकिन कोई ऐसा नहीं जिससे हर बात बता सकता था।

यूं अकेले से मेरे जीवन में एक नया मोड़ आया जिसने मेरी जिंदगी को नयी दिशा दें दी। मेरी जिंदगी में एक लड़की आई , वो मुझसे एक क्लास छोटी थी । वो दिखने में भी बहुत अच्छी थी , वैसे उसे पहले भी देखा था लेकिन उससे कभी बात नहीं हुई और कभी उस पर इतना ध्यान भी नहीं दिया था , लेकिन जब उससे बातें होने लगी तो वो धीरे धीरे अच्छी लगने लगी, ये बात स्वाभाविक है जिससे ज्यादा बात होने लगें , जिसके साथ ज्यादा समय बिताए वो कहीं न कहीं दिल में पसंद आ ही जाती है !!

उसमें जो मुझे सबसे ज्यादा पसंद था वो थी उसकी मुस्कान , जब वो मुस्कुराती थी तब मुझे उसे देखकर बहुत ही अच्छा लगता था, मन करता था उसे बस देखता ही रहूं। इसके अलावा उसके बात करने का तरीका भी बहुत अच्छा लगा , उससे बात करके मुझे वो सुकून मिलता था जो मुझे कभी नहीं मिला । मैं उससे अपनी हर बातें शेयर करने लगा , वो भी अपनी बातें मुझे बताती थी वो जो समय था वो मेरी जिंदगी का सबसे खुबसूरत पल रहा है । हमारे बीच जो बातें होती थीं वो स्कूल बस में होती थी , बातें करते करते मुझे पता ही नहीं चलता कब समय बीत गया।

मुझे मेरी जिंदगी में जिसकी तलाश थी मुझे लगा वो मिल चुकी है। मुझे बस उसका साथ चाहिए था , दूसरों की नज़र में ये प्यार हो सकता है लेकिन मेरे लिए तो वो मेरी खुशी थी , और मैं खुश होता था उसे खुश देखकर । जब भी वो मेरे सामने होती बस उसे ही देखते रहते था ना जाने क्यूं मुझे अब जिंदगी भर के लिए उसका साथ चाहिए था , हमसफ़र बनकर नहीं बस एक अच्छी दोस्त बनकर ।

धीरे धीरे समय बीत रहा था और मेरे स्कूल का आखिरी दिन भी पास आ रहा था । मुझे ऐसा लगने लगा कि स्कूल के बाद कभी उससे मेरी मुलाकात नहीं हो सकती है मैं उससे अपने मन की बात कहना चाहता था लेकिन बहुत कोशिश करने के बाद भी नहीं कह सका क्योंकि मेरी हिम्मत नहीं हो रही थी उससे कुछ कहने की । फिर वो दिसंबर का महीना आया जिसकी 21 तारीक को मैंने बहुत हिम्मत करके अपनी मन की बातें एक कागज़ में लिखकर उसे सौंप दी। बस वही एक गलती ने मुझे वापस वहीं लाकर खड़ा कर दिया जहां पहले था। उस कागज़ को उसने पढ़ा लेकिन कुछ नहीं कहा ना ही मैंने कुछ पूछा..! जब स्कूल वापसी के समय वो मुझसे पहले घर चलें गई तो मुझे एहसास हुआ कि वो उस बात से नाराज़ हो गयी है । बस अगले दिन मैंने उससे पिछले दिन की बात के लिए माफी मांगी लेकिन उसने कुछ नहीं कहा। मैंने बहुत कोशिश की उससे बात करने की, उससे समझाने की लेकिन उसने बात करना ही छोड़ दिया। जब स्कूल का आखिरी दिन वो मिली तब भी माफी मांगी लेकिन उसने मुझे अनसुना कर दिया । उसके बाद उससे कभी बात नहीं हुई मैंने कोशिश तो जारी रखी लेकिन कुछ नहीं हुआ। शायद मैं ही अपनी बात साबित नहीं कर पाया या फिर उसने ही नहीं समझा। यह आखिरी जो पल थे वो मेरी जिंदगी का सबसे बुरा अनुभव रहा है , अब भी कभी कभी उसकी याद आती है लेकिन अब कुछ नहीं हो सकता । वो खुश हैं मेरे लिए वही काफ़ी है!

"किस्मत का खेल था ये बस, जहां से शुरू हुआ वहीं खत्म हो गया, अकेला था अकेला ही रह गया "

Rishi Singh

Rishi Singh - I'm a soldier from Indian Armed Forces. I write stories and quotes. I'm from Mathura, Uttar Pradesh. Currently i'm living in kashmere gate, Delhi.

Instagram ID: - dreamy_rishii

Dosti Wala Pyaar

Phone haath mein liye main aaj bhi yehi soch raha hu.. Ki tumhare or apne baare mein likhna kis mod se shuru karu.... Yeh baat hai tab ki jab main 5th class mein new school mein aya tha... Or kuch din baad tumne bhi usi school mein admission liya tha... Wo tumhari pehli jalak... Mujhe tumhara deewana kar gyi thi... Kehna toh chahata tha but himmat nhi kar saka.. Agar mujhe pta hota ki 7th class main tumhara wo accident ho jayega toh main tumhe pehle hi sab kuch bol deta.. Sab kuch... But... Jab hum 6th class mein aye.. Tab mene class mein baki sab bacho ko toh bta diya.. But tumhe btane se mna kar diya... Or monitor ki baat toh wo wese bhi mante the toh tumhe kisi ne nhi btaya... Fir tumhe roz yuhi dekhna... Or yaad hai.. Jab tumne dance competition mein hissa liya tha.. Tab class baankk karke music room ke gate se tumhe chupke se dance karta dekhna... Mano jese main tumhare bagal mein hi dance kar raha hu.... Kehna toh hamesa se chahta tha ki kitna.. Jyada chahne laga hu main tumhe... But yeh himmat hume sirf gusse mein aati h.. Pyar mein toh sirf sarm Or dar lagta h... Yun toh bohot bahaadur tha main.. But uske saamne naa jaane kya ho jata tha mujhe... Usko samne ata dekh... Mere haatho ka yun kap kapaana... Jese wo jaanbhuj kar mere saamne aayi ho.. Usse yun nazre churana... Or kabhi kabhi toh... Lunch ke waqt bhi tum meri taraf ese hi dekhti thi na.. Jese tumhe sab pta ho... Ha to kehti kyu nhii... Tum toh sabse samajhdaar ho na... Fir yeh sab kyu nhi samjhtii..... Or ese hi waqt guzarta chala gya... Or hum 7th class mein aa gye... But khaas hum yeh new class mein aate hi nhi... Hum wese hi wahi rehte... Waqt wese hi ruk jata... April march... Bhi yuhi guzar gye... Fir aate aate january bhi aa gya.. Or fir.. Wo manhus... Month... 27th february 2013.. Haa yaad hai wo date mujhe aaj bhi... 2:45 p.m. humari chutti lag-bhag.. 2:40 par ho jaya karti thi.. Or fir jab 2:45 par hum

baahar the.. Tab... Tumhara wo accident... Mano jese uss bus se tumhari nhi... Meri takkar hui ho... Tumhe dekh dekh kar idhar udhar chilana... Wo sab... Akho se ojhal hi nhi ho raha tha.... Fir kuch din yuhi... Guzar gye.... Ha... Sabne kaha bhulne ki kosis karo.. But main... Mene toh pyar kiya tha tumse... Kese bhul jata main tumhe....

Din bitee..... Mahine bite.... Saal bhi bittee.... Din tha... Garmiyo ki chutti se ek din pehle ka... 28 April 2015... Haa... Mere Papa military mein the...Toh ab unka transfer... U.P. mein aa gya tha... Hume bhi wo school chordh kar jana pada.... Ab new school... New class... Haa meri 9th class... Ab na toh main pehle ki tarah.. Ladkiyo se baat karta tha.. Or na hi... Jyada ghumta tha... Bas... School jata Or wapas aa jata... Ese hi... Class 10th bhi guzar gyi.. Ab main 11th class mein aa gya tha.. Iss baar bhi school new tha... Or haa... Iss school mein mene dost toh bnaye... But sirf ladke... School ke principal sir ne... Ladkiyo ki classes upar jo kar rakhi thi... Or humari... Niche... Hume toh yeh tak nhi pta tha ki.. Humari class mein ladkiya kitni h....

Aaj wahi date h... 27th february 2018.... Aaj mujhe school se direct tuition jana tha.. Toh mene school ki dusre route ki bus mein beth gya.. Haaa... Aaj mene use dekha.... Haa use... Jisko dekhne ke baad... Meri akhee.... Khuli ki khuli reh gyi... Haa... Wo wahi thii... Wahiii tum akanksha jesi kese ho..... Ab main uske aage waali seat par beth gya.. Or yuhi.. Idhar udhar ko baate karne laga......

Iss mulakat ke baad humari jaan pehchan social media par hui.... Main toh tumhe dekhne ke liye.. Subha se hi.. Watercooler ke pass pani bharne ke bahane khada ho jaya karta.. Or jab tumhari bus aati.. Main ek dum se hadbda kar tumhe dekhta orfir waha se gayab ho jata... Haa aksar dhant toh padhti thi.. Ki paani bharne mein itni der kese but main hamesa wala juth bol deta... Ki line lambi thi... Jabki unhe bhi pta hota ki subha subha line nhi lagti....Or ab.. Hum ache dost hai... Aziz dost... Haa.. Usko nhi pta... Ki mere dil mein kya

hai... But wo sirf mujhe dost manti hai... Sirf dost... Hum roz ki baate karte... Apni haar choti badi baate ek dusre ko btate the.... Dheere dheere hum or bhi gehre dost ban gye... Ab mene use akanksha ke baare mein sab bta diya hai... Usko bohot dukh hua mere baare mein sunn kar... Aaj usne mujhe uske boyfriend ke baare mein bhi bta diya.... Mera aaj din... Mano jese main fir akela ho gya... Aaj 13 february 2019 raat ke 11 bje the.... Or usko esa laga ki mere dil mein uske liye kuch hai... Toh usne kasam dekar puch liya.... Ab mujhe bhi sab btana pada.... Usne mujhse haa nhi ki kyuki wo uske boyfriend se pyar jo karti thi..... But jab bhi sad hota wo samjh jati thi.. Pta nhi kase use pta chal jata Or wo haalpuchne ke liye call kar liya karti.. Butmain badi safai se jhuth toh bol deta.. But wo mera juth yuhi pakad liya karti... Or haaa uske muh se jutha sunna.. Mujhe be-had pasand h....But main toh janta tha wo ladka timepass kar raha hai.. Wahi.. Uska boyfriend Toh 13 march 2019 ko mene uske samne uske boyfriend ka sach le aya.... Aab wo or bhi jyada dukhi h.. Sochta hu mene koi galti toh nhi kardi.. Uske boyfriend ka sach uske samne laa kar... But usne jab kaha ki thank you rishi.. Toh mujhe yakin hua ki haa... Mene sahi kiya hai... Or aab mene kaha hain main karunga... Tumhara intezar.. Jab tak tumhe bhi mujhse pyar nhi ho jata....!!
Intezaar Mein Waqt bohot muskil se kat ta hai.. Na.. Mano lamho ko rok rakha ho kisi ne...
Or wese bhi.. Kisi bhi rishte mein.. Pyaar se jaruri hai.. Sabr or samjh.. Toh main yeh intezaar karna kese chordh du... Tumne kabhi sidhe mna bhi toh nahi kiya. .

Pavithra Mohanraj

Pavithra Mohanraj is a English tutor in Coimbatore. She is a Biotechnology graduate and also certified from Cambridge University for BEC course. Her father and tutors are the main reason for the write ups. They encouraged her to write what hits her mind. Later, she started to write rhyming quotes, the lesson she used to learn daily in her life.

(1)

Lots of pressure will make a diamond. Like that, today's sweat, tomorrow's sweet. We can't afford anything easily. Have to work hard for comfortable life. If we depend everyone for everything, then we should bend till our end. In this world, if you want to build an empire for you, have to work hard. You will get lot of disturbance. Many will come forward to gift problems for you. They will push you to the trouble pool. They will make your eyesland as dry land. They will make you to hate your life. But you should not accept anything as permanent. Just concentrate in your goal and move on. Nothing can't fade you, if you are strong in your goals. Do what your heart says and move on based on that. Sure you will reach success. First they will laugh at you, then they will watch you and later they will follow you. Keep this in your mind, all followers are not your fans, they may follow you to fool you. Some good hearts are waiting for you. You may meet them while walking in your destination road. Live a life to inspire others. Be a legend. Legends life will end but their stories won't end. Don't advertise your next move before completing that. Nevermind to the barking dogs. Don't hurry anything, slow process won't low your progress. Join to the people who have mindset like you. Be an ambitious legend forever. Think good, do good, you will get everything as good. Blindly don't do anything. First learn and then earn. Hence, let your ray to pave the way.This piece of advice is from my life for you people.

(2)

This is for all females. Dear ladies, don't waste your time and life for useless things. Cherish your moments. You will be a doll till your school. Then have to start your practice to live in this strange world. All are not your father or brother. They both are your guardian angels. All can't guard you. For every female, five guys are important for their life. They are dad, brother, friend, husband and son or son - in - law. If we get these five guys perfectly, we are the lucky female in the world. There are no good or bad people in the world. People change according to the situation. If we understood that, your life will be smooth. Dear Angel, laugh with many but don't trust any. Too much trust will rust you. Don't shower too much love and care, because that may hurt you if you didn't get what you give. Stay loyal until you're real comes. People will see you as a treasure and treat you as a tissue. If like that happens, don't worry we can recycle the paper, why we can't recycle our life. Monsters are also their in human makeup. Don't trust, their doll words may dark your world. Only you can care yourself. If you get a person to care you, you're lucky. Test them before starting their role in your life. If there is a dusk, there will be a dawn. If there is rain, there will be a sunshine. If today you are sad, tomorrow you will be happy. Face the problem, stay strong. Bend the one who tries to end you. If they get, that you're scared, they will rule. Don't give space for that. Always remember, for every action, their is an equal and opposite reaction.

Annawasha Naskar

As an aspiring writer, living the world of creativity of Wonder. Has some super power on her hand, moving out tge magical wand.
Insta_handle: sunheri_tiliyaan

Passioned Wala Love

It's your favorite na, then "why are you crying?" he said while he keeping his hand on my face. I immediately hid my face from him. He changes the music on the TV and I lifted my head to look at the TV screen. "Phir bhi who lamhe lete aana, aadhe aadhure se jo chute the, tare bhi who saare leete aana, jo humne dekha tha ki toote the" when this line came my tears was ready to flow from my chubby cheek and welting his t-shirt. After that he changes the song and "Ab phirse jab baarish hogi tere yaad mujhko aayegi, aayegi". Suddenly he stuck up and tears came from his eye. I picked him up in my arms and crabbled him like a "Baby".

"Shh---ssss---hhhhh----ssss--hhhhh don't cry baby, I'm not going anywhere, and I'm with you". "Nhi jaa rhi hoon hamesha rhungi tumhare paas" said by me consoling him. He wrapped me in his arms tightly than earlier and his face behind my neck. There were some tears from my side also, no not the tears of sadness it was the tears of happiness of our bonding. I'm so happy that here is someone who scared to lose me, who love me so deeply and know my feeling than me.

While hugging I thank to the God to bring us together and gifted me as "HIM".

Krishna Tangariya

Krishna Tangariya iam from haldwani/bageshwar, Uttrakhand.i am not studying.My hobby is writing nd many more.Iam motivated from my life nd all that i has experienced..

PTA HAI (Logo Ki Sachai)

Jhutii hasii pe chalra jahan h,
harr koi banna chahta mahan h.
Koi na koi mooh m faste jaa rahe,
galat kam krr k frr pachta rahe.
Pheet peche yaro sbb h bolte,
samne se har koi hath h jodte.
Gero se krne chahte h ye dosti,
yaroo ki yarii inne lagti koklii.
Pattar marte dusro pe ye ginn k,
bhul gye h shyd khud kaach k ghar h inn k.
Bolte apne appko aag h,
kuch samay baad ye khudd hi khaak h.
Choti inki sochh h,dimag m mooch h,Darti pe ye ek bojj h.
Ye sbb saap h krrte rahete paap h,
dusro ko galat bole prr khud jhoota inka baap h..

PTA HAI (Desh Ki Sachai)

Dahej k liye aurto ko marte,
jisam noch noch k kaat te.
Ladkiyo k sath khel k bolte khudko cool h,
bhul gye h shyd inke pass v ek sudar fhul h.
Jhoote wade krr k khud satywadi banta h,
dekti h sbb prr firr v chup h janta h.
Kisano pe hasta ye garibo ko lachar batata h,
ek wqat khana na mile tho ghar ko sar pe utata h.
Pyar m jaan dene vale lgte innhe toofan ,
Dekk apni bharat maa k liye kitne laal hue kurban.
Seema pe tainat apne yaar h,
bta do sbb ko ki apna desh hi apna pyar h.
Jawaani sari nashe m barbaad h,
kon kyy kahega inne ye sbb tho aajad h.
Innhe bss paisa hi dikta h,
sochte rahe ki mera ghar kitne m bikta h.
Ghar valo se banai inne bahut durii,
Galat kam krrna shock h na h inki majboorii...

Ms. Mrunal R Hatwar

She is a student nurse at MKSSS nursing Nagpur and young writer.

अभी तो सोचा था....

अभी तो सोचा था
अभी तो समझा था,
जो मेरे लिए जमी आसमां एक कर देते है;
उनके दिन का चैन
और रातो का सुकून यूहीं नहीं गया था।

अभी तो सोचा था
अभी तो समझा था,
की, उनके सर के बाल सफेद
और पैर की हड्डियां यूहीं नहीं टूटी थी।

अभी तो सोचा था
अभी तो समझा था,
की उन्होंने अपने लिए कुछ भी नहीं
पर मेरे लिए सब कुछ दिया था।

अभी तो सोचा था
अभी तो समझा था,
की मेरे सुखो के लिए
खुद सीखो से वंचित रेहेना
उन्होंने कैसे किया था।

अभी तो सोचा था
अभी तो समझा था,
की मै खाऊ या ना खाऊ
पतिले में चावल कैसे बच जाता था।

अभी तो समझा है,

की ये सब मां -बाप के सिवा
किसी और से ना हो पता।

की ये सब मां -बाप के सिवा
किसी और से ना हो पता।

डॉ निरंकुश विनायक खुबालकर

डॉ निरंकुश विनायक खुबालकर, "नीर" तखल्लुस से लिखते हैं. खेल और संगीत से गहरा लगाव हैं उन्हें..

पेशे से जैवविज्ञानी, वनस्पतिशास्त्री, शिक्षक, ट्रेकिंग और निसर्ग में रुचि रखते.. साथ में हिन्दी, मराठी और अँग्रेजी में लेखन, वैज्ञानिक विषयों में भाषण, सामाजिक कार्यों में योगदान. कविता एवं स्फुट लेखन इनके प्रिय विषय.. पिछले कई सालों से काव्य प्रकाशित करते हैं...

इश्क़ में तुम बिन नहीं रहना..

कहते हैं ना, अब भी वक़्त हैं, सम्भल जाओ, वरना..
समझदारी इसी में जो जानता वक़्त के साथ चलना..

हर कोई, कभी-न-कभी कहता, कितना हमने सहना..
हर कोई अक्सर चाहता हैं, किसी के प्यार में पड़ना..

और कहता रहता, इश्क़ में अब तुम बिन नहीं रहना..
कुछ भी हो जाय, उसे मंज़ूर होता हैं, पागल बनना..

इश्क़ की दीवानी चाहती, बनूँ उसके गले का गहना..
दिल दिया हैं तुझे, चाहूँगी अब तेरे ही दिल में रहना..

ज़िंदगी के सफ़र में साथ जीना और साथ ही मरना..
"नीर" के मन में उठता एक सवाल "अब क्या कहना"..

Chanchal Punyani

Chanchal Punyani was born in Nagpur, Maharashtra. She is a kind and sweet girl who likes to help people.She currently studies in Banglore.

A Dreadful Day Of My Life

A dark sunny day, dark of my life and sunny for the mother Earth, when a seven year old girl had to enter a lavishing hospital with her mom and dad to identify which disease has found heaven in her mom.

Three pounding hearts entered a seven storey building. After two hours of wait in extreme anxiousness, our turn to meet the doctor came. Doctor provided us with the best service and did all the tests like MRI, CT scan etc to diagnose the illness. After all this, we came to know that there is 75 percent blockage in a valve of her heart and it will be good if it is operated today itself. A fast decision of operating her was taken. But I, being a girl of very small age couldn't understand anything. I just knew that my mom will be operated now. Everything was just moving for me, going up and down from this floor to that floor. Finally, my mom was taken into operation theatre. I was told by dad to sit in the waiting area. Complying to him, I said yes, but I had no idea, where my dad is going, where is the operation theatre, how much time will it take for the operation to happen etc. What I just saw was my mom being taken on a stretcher, and this was enough to bring tears in my eyes. After Two hours of continuous fear, anxiousness and negative thoughts, I just got little relaxed when dad entered the waiting room and again we played the game of floors.

Conclusion came that operation wasn't successful.

Nawab Azhar

Engineer
Insta id- hashtag_azhar_ahmed_

(1)

जिस तरह फिसलती है रेत मुट्ठी से वैसे
तेरी यादों से आज़ाद हो जाऊं
और मैं अकेला यमुना सा कब तक बहुँ
कोई गंगा सी मिल जिससे संगम हो के इलाहाबाद हो जाऊ

और दिल के हाल लिखने लगा हूँ मैं ज़रा मुस्कुरा तो दो
तुम ही तो चाहती थी न की मैं बर्बाद हो जाऊं

कफ़न में ही दफ़न हो जाती है हसरते दिल की
तुम जो हो रोने को तैयार तो मैं आज ही मर जाऊं

वो जबरन याद आते है तुम उन्हें बताओ तो अज़हर
है आदत उनकी याद आने की के जब तक मैं परेशा न हो जाउ

ये आंखे अगर इज़हार कर पाए
तो आसान दिल का काम हो जाये
की अपनी बाते लफ़्ज़ों में कहने में नीलाम न हो जाऊं

भले ही चाहता हु मैं मगर ये जनता हु मैं
ये कहानी हैं महोब्बत की मुकम्मल हो नही सकती

और धड़कनो की रफ्तार अचानक ही नही बढ़ती है
ये है उसकी मेहरबानी की वो घर मे ही सवारती है

और जो दुप्पटा सर से यूं सरक जाए
तो तमाम महफ़िलो में कत्ले आम सा मच जाए

Manoj Agarwal

I live what I am, I cannot pretend what I am not. I am a very sensible person with lots of happiness
Insta id- @dil_se_zubaa_tak

Let's Talk About Good And Bad Memories

Hello! Guys I am writing this just because I want to write this, so the story is totally of mine, but it is a
real life story where me, Oh! First of all let me introduce myself. Hello! I am Mohan from a small town
named Tinsukia which is situated in the Assam, and any I am from a middle class family of town with
some dreams and big expectations. My expectation is so big that from whoever I expect something my
expectation is to get spoiled.
But luckily, by the grace of God I got a friend, and who is a brother to me his name, and is Rohan we are
together since last ten years we are together. We are something more than a friend but not less than
brother.
Our bond is so good, that he introduced one of his friend named Princess to me. So that I get
committed.
I was so influenced by her that I ignored my official work as well as my carrier and also my daily routine.
Rohan is so smart that he created a what's app for group, and so that texting her direct doesn't make
her feel that I am a cheap guy.
We started chatting in fact late night calls were also allowed after a month. I I asked her for date many
times and we used to go together and she never denied of anything I offered on her birthday, I also
planned a surprise for her and I am had booked entire restaurant for her. I asked her friend to make her
come in the location where I planned a surprise for her. She came there but just for 15 minutes. I was so
happy and cheerful after seeing her. After few days, I went to her place and meet her family. They were

so understanding and socialized. I was shocked, I decided to accept them as my own from that day. I was

having two mothers, and in fact for me she is still my mother but not officially.

So every thing was normal and session of festival started just after the year pass, I me and my friend

decided to visit her place on holi. Her house is very far from town but still for her I went there on the

festival day, "She was their, she was smiling my heart was their and I was crying", my tears were the

blessing and her happiness was the prayer. I was happy and cheerful after celebrating my festival, I went

home with thought and with her color which she putted on my face. I was not accepting the bath, and

but have too. That's the bloody truth.

After everything I proposed her formally but she denied not of she was committed, but she was not

ready for relationship. Everything was good and fine for me it was worship I was devote of her.

I did everything not because I want relationship but I want her to be happy time phase with million of

chat and a day came when I get to know that she was committed with a guy, with whom she was started

chatting for last one month.

She never said to me. All my pains were very personal still it is personal and I know it will be personal

that's all.

I am not blaming her but I don't want to see her face again.

Reason will be known to you but not now. It will be enclosed in Part-II. So guys wait for Part-2. The story

of mine cannot be enclosed to in one, and it has many parts

Manpreet Kaushal

Student of B.CA, lives in Punjab,
The writer who think different from the world

बहन

कौन कहता है बुर्के मे लोग safe होते है,
मैंने सुना है दुबई मे भी rape होते है,,

अपनी बहन तो बहन दूसरे की बहन माल,
कर रखी है आजकल के लड़कों ने भी कमाल,
कपड़े rape का कारन है तो कपड़े बहन के भी same होते है,,
कौन कहता है बुर्के मे लोग safe होते है,
मैंने सुना है दुबई मे भी rape होते है,,

रिश्तों की कदरें सिर्फ़ कबरों मे होती है,
चावल से छोटी लोगों की औकात छोटी है,
गरीब को यार बोलने मे ये लोग shame होते है,,
कौन कहता है बुर्के मे लोग safe होते है,
मैंने तो सुना है दुबई मे भी rape होते है,,

मोबाइल ने बच्चों को माँ बाप से इतना दूर कर दिया है,
आजकल पैसे ने हमे रिश्ते निभाने पे मजबूर कर दिया है,
कौशल लोग तो पैसा देखकर दूसरों के slave होते है,,
कौन कहता है बुर्के मे लोग safe होते है,
मैंने तो सुना है दुबई मे भी rape होते है,,

Atif Nawab

Name: ATIF NAWAB
I am from ANANTNAG KASHMIR
Insta id- atifnawab1366

(1)

1. Always maintain your simplicity, because these are only simply people who live smoothly
2. Always put a smile on yours face, do you know someone smile because of you
3. Let's plants some flowers in this barren land today whose fragrance perfumes the whole city
4. If you want to live yours life peacefully, beautify your character.
5. Pain of wounds of others is not felt,
until the wounds are inflected on self

(2)

1. We were lost in the darkness of a lie, a small light disclosed the truth & everything became bright & clear
2. Don't love such people, who describe your good in front of you & evil behind your back.
3. Don't be discouraged by your disability, because God has made you the most special.
4. How beautiful are the autumn movements, but what we do no is that it is the season when the leaves die.
5. Remove your bad habits if you want a stress free life.

Aman Sharma

Aman Sharma is from Patna, Bihar. He obtained a Bachelor's Degree in Mathematics from renowned Anugrah Narayan College. He likes traveling, reading, and playing badminton.
In higher secondary, he was going through a dark time, and then he developed an epiphany towards writing, to speak his heart out.

The Girl With A Golden Heart

The mortal smoking close by Full Street
Endowed by an English Rose, background elite;
Coping himself with a rough road
She had put him up as true–blue, without load;
Worse luck, an accident tearing his shoulder apart,
He refused the help, she offered.
Tears rolling down her cheeks but lips reserved,
And eyes saying that aloud, breaking the heart.
Clouds of reminiscing flashed upon his eyes,
"The hotel meet, where they initiated, without lies;
She, a raging beauty but he, a torn mess
Making both of them feel bless;
Before leaving they swapped their Facebook handle,
After few days, she boarded the cupid train but
He, still, walking the same path of coax
Sorry with a cause, telling her the differences in the candle.
A month of their friendship shattered by love - God;
Leaving them outcast, not from the same squad"
The thud of pain making his return to the present,
Agreeing for help like an errant;
Accompanied by her, her mother, and silence,
The car stopped by a clinic, stitching the wound,
Before he would offer she already paid for it,
Requesting him to get back in the car, without violence.
Dropping him nearby she cleared the air
Called for medication and uttered, please take care;
A week after, she appeared again in front of his college
To get stitches undone, like a book of knowledge;
During the Ride, they made a chat
About everything, especially why she admired him,
After the treatment, She produced her last words
'I'll always love you my dear brat.'

Sarvesh Kumar

Inside talk with pen

(1)

जिंदगी बड़ी अजीब है
जिने भी दो
ऐ जाम मेरा है
अब मुझे पीने भी दो
जो घाव दिये हो
अब उन्हें सिलने भी दो
पाव के छाले अभी ठण्डे भी नहीं हुए
की तेरे अपने फ़साने शुरू हो गये
दो वक्त का न सही
एक वक्त की ही रोटियाँ तोड़ने भी दो

(2)

खुला है मौसम लम्बी है राते
चलो करते है चाय की चुस्कीयो   पर बाते
वो बाते भी कुछ खास होगी
जैसे अदरक वाली चाय होगी

Izhar

Izhar Alam is a writer from Bihar, currently living in Delhi.
He is persuing B.Pharm from AIMT, Greater Noida,
His first book as a co-author is CHIMERA An Illusion,
Udaan Sapno Ki, Inspiration and many more to come.
He loves to write about love and betrayal, but sometimes write
something different if he feels he can write something good
about it.
He started writing in 2015

(1)

तुम हमराह बन तो जाओ मेरे,
तुम्हे हमसफर बना लेंगे।

ज़िन्दगी गर बिताना है अकेले में,
तुम्हे एक शहर बना देंगे।

कोई कमी रह जाए अगर,
मेरे शहर बनाने में तो बता देना।

खुद के ख्वाब ना सही,
तुम्हारा शहर पूरा बना देंगे।

(2)

मैं सबर भी करूं और फल भी ना पाऊं,
बताओ ये भी कोई इन्साफ है क्या।

तुम मेरे ना हुए चलो कोई बात नहीं,
तुम रकीब के हो गए ये कोई अच्छी बात है क्या।

Srishti Rani Panda

This is Srishti Rani Panda a small town girl from Rayagada odisha who aspires to become a news anchor...For her writing is the best way of expressing one's feeling... She wants to bring a sweet smile in her mom's face...

Yes, It's My Story:-

The pathetic phase of my life, which I do not want to
memorise,
Where my dreams just vanished, but nightmares turned real,
Where my lips were stiched , but my soul screamed mere,
My friends became foes and my foes turned more,
My only soulmate ditched me and no one was near,
Taunted by my family, Trusted by no one,
I felt myself in a grave and with none,
Loneliness turned into my mate and that to too honest,
Persistently greeted the suicidal thoughts in my mind,
I weighed a plastic surgery smile on my face,
Alive from apperance, but dead from inside,
Chaos and scars replaced me in my life,
This phase I don't want to memorise,
It still haunts me day and night like a spirit,
A phase - good or bad, I still didn't categorise,
Because it taught me something which I again want to revise.

Tannu Sahay

Tannu Sahay is the author of............ Of this book. She was born and brought up in Muzaffarpur, Bihar
She went to Prabhat Tara School and is now pursuing her class 12th from Holy Mission Sr. Sec. School, Muz. She is fond of reading different types of poetries and books.Her curiousity and opnion for certain things taking place around her motivated her to express her thoughts in the form of poetries

(1)

मिली थी ज़िंदगी किसी के
काम आने के लिए

लेकिन ज़िंदगी बीत गयी
काग़ज कमाने में

क्या करोगे इतना पैसा कमाकर
ना कफन में जेब है
न कब्र में अलमारी
और यह मौत के फ़रिश्ते तो
रिश्वत भी नहीं लेते.....

(2)

वो कल जिसे हमने देखा नहीं ,
उसकी ख्वाइश में ये ज़िंदगी दौड़ती चली जाती है।

लेकिन वो कल जो बीत गया,
उसकी याद आज को खूबसूरत बनाती है।।

(3)

ख़र्च कर दिया मैंने ख़ुद को ,
जिन अपनों के लिए ।

उन अपनों ने तो ,
एक बार पलट कर देखना भी ज़रूरी नहीं समझा हमें हमारी बर्बादी
पर ।।

(4)

दुनिया भर के रिश्तों का बोझ उठा के चला था
क्या पता था मुसीबत के वक्त ख़ुद को अकेला पाऊँगा

(5)

जिसके हाथों में
छाला होगा

यकीनन दर्द उस ने ही
पाला होगा

(6)

ख़ुशी आपकी, हँसाता है जमाना
दर्द आपके, रुलाता है जमाना

(7)

कौन कहता है दर्द इंसान को
कुछ नायाब तोहफ़ा अदा नही फरमाते

ये दर्द तो
इंसान को दुबारा ज़िंदगी जीने का हौसला सीखा जाते हैं

Apeksha Vilas

Apeksha Vilas is an Interior & Landscape Designer and also an aspiring Architect. She loves to write and read poetries, watch stand-up comedy and have special interest in styling. She has her own online clothing store.
Ig: Apeksha_vilas

Endless Love

My love for you was boundless but you didn't cared to value it.
After you destroyed my heart with your actions and words, All I did was cried all night.
A particular phase of my life was tough to handle , but after loosing you, My heart gave me that lost laugh in bundle.
The moments we shared were another fun for you, but it still gives me goosebumps when I remember them.
One part in my heart will always remember you , because once it had no-one but you.
Doesn't matter how much you love a person , they going to leave you one day or other.
Life would challenge you in each and every phase , but you need to be stronger every time than before.
No, I don't blame you for things you did ,
My love for you was, is and will be indeed.

Wise Choice

This tears rolling down is a sign of hurt you're facing today , let it go , its a sign of making you strong.
The situation you're in today is a phase , with time it will be vanished.
The problems you're facing is a sign , that god wants you to be strong enough.
The heart which got demolished by a person was just to build your charecter more wise and strong.
Heartbreak is good , if you look at it in a positive way it made you so strong as a person.
Thank to the person who made you strong enough, to look at the world in better way.
Bad things are part of life , accepting , moving and learning is a wise person choice.
The love you gave will reciprocate soon.

K. Karthik

Karthik is from Chennai, Tamil Nadu. He is working in private concern in chennai after completing mechanical engineering. He loves to Sing, play cricket and football, write down feelings as short poem mostly and likes to be kind, honest, friendly and polite in nature.

"A Little smile can bring a positive change in others." Let' smile and keep spreading happiness.

Joy Of Giving:

Life is all about enjoying our happenings
Around us even it is a smaller one, taking it to our
Heart and enjoy the moment every minute in life.
Once I was travelling in a bus, Old man was asking everyone
in the bus to give donations by issuing the slip of the temple
opening ceremony, he looked in dirty dress and a strange look
too.
Last seat on the bus, some college girls were sitting in groups
and had commented on him, started to laugh together, he came
to me and I just checked my pocket and found 100 rupees,
without hesitation I gave that money to him.
He looked at me once before receiving and I smiled. He just
sent to those girls again and started to express his feelings don't
comment bad and make fun on people like me once I had great
life now everything lost, so I become like that and he turned
on me, telling guy who sitting over there, just looked at me and
giving money whatever comes from pocket without thinking.i
am in state of no words by this way of act, long living my kind
hearted men and he stated to walk away from bus. That
moment in the bus everyone looked at me surprisingly and I
felt happiness that I never experienced anywhere in life.
The joy of giving is absolutely divine like thing in life.

Priyanka Yadav

Currently i'm persuing under graduation from Delhi University.

"जान"

बहुत खास हो तुम मेरे लिए
ये हर बार जताना ज़रूरी तो नहीं,
तुम्हें दिन रात अपनी दुआओं में मांगती हूं
इस तरह बेवक्त दुआएं मांगना किसी गैर के लिए तो नहीं,
तुम्हें अपने हर लम्हें, हर ख़्याल में साथ रखती हूं
इस तरह तुम्हें ख़ुद में समा लेना बेवजह तो नहीं,
तुम्हारे जरा सा उदास होने पर परेशान हो जाती हूं
इस तरह तुम्हारे लिए परेशान होना कोई ढोंग तो नहीं,
तुम्हारी हर छोटी बड़ी खुशी का ध्यान रखती हूं
इस तरह तुम्हारा ख्याल रखना कोई दिखावा तो नहीं,
तुम्हारे सपनों को अपना समझकर पूरा करती हूं
इस तरह तुम्हारी हो जाना किसी ख़्वाब से कम तो नहीं,
ख़ुद को भूल तुम्हारे लिए फिक्रमंद रहती हूं
इस तरह की बेख्याली किसी अंजान के लिए तो नहीं,
तुम्हारे हर अच्छे बुरे वक्त में तुम्हारे साथ खड़ी रहती हूं
इस तरह तुम्हारी हमराही होना कोई मज़ाक तो नहीं,
तुम्हारे हर राज़ को अपने दिल में दफ़न रखती हूं
इस तरह तुम्हारी हमराज बनना कोई आसान तो नहीं,
तुम्हारी एक झलक देखने को अक्सर बेकरार हो जाती हूं
इस तरह तुम्हारा दीदार करना कोई पागलपन तो नहीं,
तुम्हारी तस्वीरों को अक्सर घंटों एकटक निहारती रहती हूं
इस तरह ख़ुद को तुम्हारे करीब महसूस करना आसान तो नहीं,
तुम्हारी याद में बहते हुए आंसुओं को अक्सर छुपा लेती हूं
इस तरह बेवक्त रोना कोई शौक़ तो नहीं,
तुम्हारे लिए अक्सर अपनों से खफा हो जाती हूं
इस तरह बेवजह की नाराज़गी कोई अच्छी तो नहीं,
हा! माना कि बेहिसाब मोहब्ब्त है हमें तुमसे
पर ये हर वक्त जताना ज़रूरी तो नहीं...!!

''ज़िंदगी''

कहने को तो एक शब्द है
पर असल मे इसके रंग तो अनेक है,
कुछ अच्छे, कुछ बुरे, कुछ खट्टे, कुछ मीठे
कभी अपनों के साथ तो कभी अपनों से जुदा,

बस ऐसे ही कुछ लम्हों का नाम है ज़िंदगी
जिन्हें हर शख्स अपनी ज़िन्दगी में जीना चाहता है,

कुछ ऐसे ही लम्हों से मेरी ज़िन्दगी भी संजी सवरी है
जहां कुछ लोग तो दिल के बहुत ही करीब है तो वही कुछ लोग दिल
के दूर दूर तक भी नहीं,
जिनमें कुछ ने ढाल बन मेरे बुरे वक्त में मेरा साथ दिया
तो कुछ ने बहाने बनाकर फासले कर लिए,
पर हां! मैं शुक्रगुजार दोनों की ही हूं
क्योंकि अगर साथ देने वाले ना होते तो शायद मेरा यूं खुश रह पाना
मुश्किल हो जाता,
और अगर ये साथ ना छोड़ते तो मेरा इन पर विश्वास और वक्त दोनों
ही ज्यादा लग जाता
जिसका मुझे अपने बुरे वक्त से भी ज्यादा अफ़सोस होता,
बस कुछ ऐसी ही है मेरी ज़िन्दगी...!!

Navjot Singh

Navjot singh, an aspiring author and a physiotherapist has worked on 2 projects including the famous Harry Potter fan fiction, "Harry Potter And The Curse Of The Lying Prophecy." He loves to write about nature, love and self worth.
Author can be reached on his Instagram
@the_vintage_soul

Was It Worth?

Was searching for a partner,
A garden for Gardner,
Was always all alone,
Like a classical music in a single tone,
Nothing was going very well,
What do you want oh God! Please tell,
What about appreciation i never got,
Was my work worth it or not?

Neither tried nor did i judge,
I never started a proper grudge,
Why always i am found to be guilty,
All say, i am wrong just that simply,
All the work i did is than forgot,
I started asking myself,
Was my work worth it or not?

I never knew it would be you,
All the rubbish that you threw,
Wanted and always helped you flew,
All i wanted is you to escort,
But you made me think,
Was my work worth it or not?

D A Blithe

D A Blithe is a Kashmiri Muslim writer and the poet, his philosophy of life is Islam, Qutubism, Revivalism. His real name is Danish Aslam badana and is 16 years old. He is studying in class 11th science he is from district Kupwara but is currently living in district Srinagar to continue his studies. At the age of 10 he wrote his first poem titled "Kashmir" which was based on the scenic beauty of Kashmir. Then he wrote few more poems on the same topic along with the topics of righteousness and equality. In the Year 2019 he heard about Hafeez Jalandhari's poetry book based on the Islamic history and the seerah of Prophet Muhammad Sallallahu alaihis Salam. He wrote the English poetic form of Prophet Muhammad Sallallahu alaihis Salam's seerah. He also wrote several motivational poems in order to promote Revivalism. insta id- @therealinksmith

World And Me

A young chirping bird, new to the World,
Unknown to differences of coal and gold,
When caught by a black smokey cloud
during his journey to Falconry, was amazed,
He tried to escape and sometimes cried aloud,
When got no help, he tried but failed.

A young chirping bird, during a day nap,
Sat on a hunters cage, hence lost in a trap.
On awakening, he found himself trapped,
So for help he cried here and there,
He called his mother, but no one replied.
So failed when got response from nowhere.

A young chirping bird, clashed with a Crow,
And because of young mind, refused to bow,
The crow hit him to fall on the ground.
He cried for help and his group was there,
He explained the condition, they hide all around.
He failed and cried, but learned a moral pair,

"Never wait for help, be your own hero,
And your every hundred is none without zero."

Sujit Sahebrao Pawar

#writer
#sports player
#writ up owns life
Do follow
@pawarsujit23
@victorywriter

Experience Of Life.

जमाना आज का बड़ा खराब है, उस ज़माने मे साफ़ दिल वाला आज भी मौजूद है, ना किसीका बुरा सोचना, ना किसीके बारे पीछे से बात करना. ये उसकी आदत थी, आदत ये बड़ी अच्छी थी , लोगों के लिए मतलब कि फर्माइश थी..

आया हर एक इंसान पूरा अपना मतलब कर गया,

साजिश कहीं नो रखी पीछे मुझे रखने की, फिर भी हौसला बढ़ता गया जो भी बुरा सोच रहा था उसको भी साथ लेते चला.

हर एक का यहा वजूद था, जो साथ जुड़ा काम पूरा होते ही अनजान बन गया, बोहत कम थे यहा जो मेरे जैसे जीना चाहते थे, सपने भी एक साथ एक जैसे देखा करते थे, सोचा खुद बढ़ेंगे आगे तो साथ लेके बढ़ेंगे उसे, पर यहा तो वो भी पैसों के भूखे निकले, बस अपने मतलब के लिए हमसे जुड़ गए थे.

खराब ज़माने मे कहीं गेरो से मुलाकात हुई, मीठे शब्द सुन अपनों से दूरी हो गई थी, टाइम आने पे अकेला पाया हमने खुदको, ज़माने के साथ चलना सिखाया अपनों ने, तजुर्बा मिला आंख बन भरोसे का यहा तो सब मतलबी है यारा, अब किसपे भरोसा करना.

बड़ी आसान थी जिंदगी, बीतते पलो ने डरना सिखाया, यहा चलना भी अकेला था जो हज़ारो के बीच खडा था. मिले यहा वफादार कहीं सारे जो है आज भी साथ मेरे, समय का इंतजार है वरना उन्हें भी अपना किरदार बताना है.

है यहा कहीं अच्छे, जिन्हें जिम्मेदारियों ने घेरा है वरना

वो भी आझाद थे कहीं अपने मेहखानेमे. उन्हें भी हमने कभी दुखाया नहीं जिन्होंने हर पल हमे रुलाया है.

सबक बोहत से मिले जिंदगी जीते जीते, उसे अपना अनुभव बनाते चला हर एक साप जैसे दोस्तों को हातो से अपने दूध पीलाता गया. ऐसा अनुभव दिलाता गया...

काटकसर

जमाना आज का बड़ा खराब है, उस ज़माने मे साफ़ दिल वाला आज भी मौजूद है, ना किसीका बुरा सोचना, ना किसीके बारे पीछे से बात करना. ये उसकी आदत थी, आदत ये बड़ी अच्छी थी , लोगों के लिए मतलब कि फर्मा़इश थी..

आया हर एक इंसान पूरा अपना मतलब कर गया,

साजिश कहीं नो रखी पीछे मुझे रखने की, फिर भी हौसला बढ़ता गया जो भी बुरा सोच रहा था उसको भी साथ लेते चला.

हर एक का यहा वजूद था, जो साथ जुड़ा काम पूरा होते ही अनजान बन गया, बोहत कम थे यहा जो मेरे जैसे जीना चाहते थे, सपने भी एक साथ एक जैसे देखा करते थे, सोचा खुद बढ़ेंगे आगे तो साथ लेके बढ़ेंगे उसे, पर यहा तो वो भी पैसों के भूखे निकले, बस अपने मतलब के लिए हमसे जुड़ गए थे.

खराब ज़माने मे कहीं गेरो से मुलाकात हुई, मीठे शब्द सुन अपनों से दूरी हो गई थी, टाइम आने पे अकेला पाया हमने खुदको, ज़माने के साथ चलना सिखाया अपनों ने, तजुर्बा मिला आंख बन भरोसे का यहा तो सब मतलबी है यारा, अब किसपे भरोसा करना.

बड़ी आसान थी जिंदगी, बीतते पलो ने डरना सिखाया, यहा चलना भी अकेला था जो हज़ारो के बीच खडा था. मिले यहा वफादार कहीं सारे जो है आज भी साथ मेरे, समय का इंतजार है वरना उन्हें भी अपना किरदार बताना है.

है यहा कहीं अच्छे, जिन्हें जिम्मेदारियों ने घेरा है वरना

वो भी आझाद थे कहीं अपने मेहखानेमे. उन्हें भी हमने कभी दुखाया नहीं जिन्होंने हर पल हमे रुलाया है.

सबक बोहत से मिले जिंदगी जीते जीते, उसे अपना अनुभव बनाते चला हर एक साप जैसे दोस्तों को हातो से अपने दूध पीलाता गया. ऐसा अनुभव दिलाता गया...

Payal Goswami

Payal, currently living in Delhi.
She is studying in BA 1st year. Her first book as a co-author is CHIMERA an Illusion,
Bharm, Inspiration and many more to come.
She loves to write about love and betrayal, but sometimes write something different if she feels she can write something good about it.
She started writing in 2018

इतनी सी जिंदगी मेरी....

जैसे खुले आसमान में पंछी उड़ते हैं

वैसे ही मुझे खुशियों का आसमान छूना था.....

खुद को बचपन से जिस हाल में देखा वहां से बाहर ले जाना था.........

जहां मैं और मेरा परिवार खुशी से रह सके ऐसा आशियाना बनाना था........

नादान कहो या कहो मुझे पागल

बस ऐसे ही बातें सोचा करती थी मैं

घरवालों के ताने सुन सुन कर बड़ी हुई हूं मैं

मिट्टी में खेली...... मिट्टी में बड़ी हुई हूं मैं

दोस्तों के नाम पर टोली थी मेरी........

पूरे दिन घूमना काम था मेरा........

पढ़ना, लिखना, सजना, सवरना

कहां आता था मुझे..........

बस रोज़ छोटी छोटी खुशियां बटोरा करती थी मै.....

अब नादान कहो या पागल मुझे

बस ऐसे ही किया करतीं थीं मैं

अब जब बड़ी हों गई हूं मै.....

घर कि बड़ी बेटी हूं मैं........

मुझे पराएं घर जाना है......

ये रोज़ सुनने को मिलता हैं.....

सपने देखना गलती हैं या लड़की हूं मैं ये गलती हैं मेरी

हालातों से भागना नहीं आता मुझे......

कोशिश भी ना करु मैं.....ये सबसे बड़ी गलती होंगी मेरी

छोटी सी उम्र से सपने बुनना शुरू किया था मेने.....

बंद आंखों से नहीं खुली........आंखों से सपने देखे हैं मेंने.....अपने

पापा को कड़ी धूप में काम करते देखा है मैंने..........

अपनी मां को तवे पर हाथ काले करते देखा है मैंने.....

बस ज़्यादा कुछ नहीं......उनको खुशियां देना चाहतीं हूं......

पराएं घर नहीं अपने घर जाना चाहती हूं......
बस इतनी सी जिंदगी हैं मेरी......
बस इतना सी हैं ख्वाइश मेरी......

Ravina Thadani

Ravina Thadani is from Ajmer, Rajasthan. She is studying Bsc mathematics from Aryan college. Her hobbies are reading, writing, drawing, singing and sketching and Come up with new ideas that improved things and achieved rewards. Being an introverted personality, she got a medium to express herself via writing.
insta id- @11_59_stories

1

बात बहुत पुरानी हैं। वो छुट्टियों के दिन, वो नानी का घर, वो टीवी पर रिमोट फाइट, वो विंडो वाली सीट, वो ट्रेन की सवारी, वो तेज़ हवा में उड़ते बाल।

अचानक सामने एक प्यारी सी बच्ची आई , चहरे पर ना कोई चमकान, ना ही कोई नूर । जनरल कोच (सीट नंबर 37), गुस्ते ही उसने अपना करतब दिखाना शुरू कर दिया । मैं अपनी लहरो की दुनिया से बाहर आकर उसे एकटक देखने लगी, जरा दाई बाई ओर मुड़कर देखा तो सबकी नज़रे कही और ही थी मनो कोई खोफ सा हो 'फिर पैसे मांगेगी'।

नाट्य ख़त्म कर एक उम्मीद की किरण आँखों में ले उसने अपनी कटोरी आगे की। नज़रे अभी भी मानो उसी डर से ही इजाजत नही दे रही थी । कहते है ' जेब कितनी भी ऊची क्यों न हो , गरीबो के आगे झुक ही जाती है ।' मैंने जट से उसका हाथ थामा और पापा से जिद्द करने लगी 'दो ना पापा पैसे '। पापा ने जट से मेरा हाथ खेंचा और 'ऐसो का हाथ नहीं पकड़ते ' सुनकर वोह चली गयी ।

मैं भी फिर से उन लहरों की आवाजों में घूम हो गयी पर इस बार में अकेली नही थी बल्कि हज़ारो सवालों से अंदर ही अंदर लड़ रही थी ।

' क्यों कोई इनसे बात नही करता ? क्या यह सबसे दूर रहते है ? क्यों लोग इतनी प्यारी सी बच्ची से काम कराते है? अगर मेरे से भी कोई बात न करे तोह ? मेरी भी बातो को कोई अनसुना करे तोह ? मानो उस दिन स्वयं सरस्वती मेरे मुख में विराजमान थी। स्टेशन आते ही सवालों की बरसात को पोटली मे बांध किसी कोने मे रख दिया।

कुछ सालों बाद हमारा परिवार एक छोटी सी दुनिया से बाहर निकलकर, एक नयी दुनिया मे कदम रखनें जा रहा था। वो बात कुछ एसी थी 'पापा का तबादला अजमेर हो गया'।

29 अप्रैल 2016, नए स्कूल का पहला दिन, "कहा मिलेगी 11B" बोलते ही पीछे से आवज आई 'फ़र्स्ट फ्लोर, सीधे से दाई ओर'।
मैं जट से भागी और तेज से चीलाया "May I come in, ma'am " इंट्रोडक्शन हुआ, सबसे बातचीत हुई, पहले ही दिन सबके दिलों में जगह बना ली मनो वीकेन्ड की मूवी टिकट, लोंग ड्राइव, मस्ती, मजाक सब ऑन था। कहतें है, "घेर लेते है काले बादल उस नीले गगन को, तभी पूर्णिमा का चांद अमावस्या में बदल जाता है।" धीरे धीरे कोने मे रखी पोटली की गिठान ढीली पड रही थीं, उस हसते खेलते शरीर मे मनो जंग सी पड रही थीं।

चुप चाप बस्ते को रख कोने मे बैठ जाती क्यूंकि ना ही बोलने वाले बचे थे और ना ही पूछने वाले। लंच की बेल रखते ही दबे पाव अकेले नीचे जाना, सबके ग्रुप देख आंखे भर आना। घर आकर तकिया अपनी आंखो मे रख रो पडती। शायद माँ सरस्वती सच मुच उस प्यारी सी बच्ची का दर्द महसूस करना चाहती थी। स्कूल की समुंद्र की लहरे घर तक आ रही थी फिर भी दिल को समजाती रहती "एसा कुछ नही है। रोज रात को आसूँ खुद ही टपक पडते शायद उन्हे भी अपनी दैनिक दिनचर्या का आबास सा हो गया। मन अशांत है और नियंत्रित करना कठिन है, लेकिन अभ्यास से इसे वश में किया जा सकता हैं।

29 अप्रैल 2020, फिर से वोह पल दोहराया, एक प्यारी सी बच्ची, चहरे पर ना कोई चमकान, ना ही कोई नूर । जनरल कोच (सीट नंबर 37), गुस्ते ही उसने अपना करतब दिखाना शुरू कर दिया। पर इस बार ना कोई जिद्द, ना दाई बाई ओर मुडना। बस भीनी सी मुस्कान लिए उसका करतब देखा और उसकी उम्मीद की किरण को बढ़ाते हुए, घंटो बातचीत की मानो उसे बताने का जरिया मिल गया हो और मुझे उन सवालो से आजादी।

आँखे मूंदती पंखुडिया ने

तितलियों से कल फिर मिलने का वादा लिया होगा।।
जानती हूँ, खारे बादलों में मिठास ढूंढता
वो भी सबकी तरह इस शहर में तन्हा होगा।।

Vaibhav Dev Singh

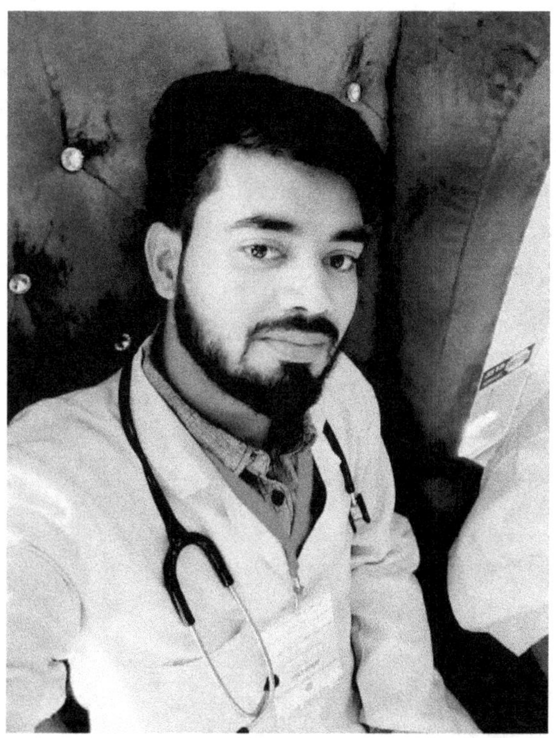

I'm from Ballia, Uttar Pradesh.
Student of Bachelor of Ayurvedic Medicine and Surgery
(B.A.M.S.)
Hobbies - Singing, Writing
Instagram - @jazbaat.in
YouTube Channel - Vaibhav Dev Singh

"पिता जी"

अग्रणी होकर हर काम में आपका आगे आना
किसी भी काम को जब तक खुद न करें
विश्वास न आना
कभी ये आदतें मुझे बुरी लगती थी
पिता जी आपकी ये आदतें मुझे अच्छी लगती हैं।।
मुझे वो दिन याद है
जब मैं आपके बांह पर अपना सिर रखकर सोता था ,
जब आपको दर्द होता, आप रोते थे, मैं भी रोता था।
हां बचपन में लिखावट के लिए मार बहुत खाई है
यही वजह है मेरी Hand writing अच्छी बन आई है।
कभी ये आदतें मुझे बुरी लगती थी
पिता जी आपकी ये आदतें मुझे अच्छी लगती है।।
जब आपने मुझे एक बात की खातिर
नए साल को एक जवाब की खातिर
मुझे गले लगाया था।
एक दिन आप साइकिल से जा रहे थे कहीं
मुझे झूंसी लगा
मैं रोते - रोते दौड़कर पीछे आया था।
वो दिन भी याद है
जब मैनें आपको ये बताया था
रात 3 बजे जब मुझे भूख ने सताया था
किया नमकीन खतम मैं
फिर आपको खूब हसाया था।
उस दिन की बात मैं कैसे भूल सकता हूं
जब मैं रजाई गट्टर के नीचे आया था
फिर आपने चाचा के साथ मिलकर
ड्राइवर को खूब बजाया था।
आपने हर समय मेरे लिए खाना कम खाया है

कहीं मुझे कम न पड़ जाए
आपने मुझे ज्यादा खिलाया है।
कभी ये आदतें मुझे बुरी लगती थी
पिता जी आपकी ये आदतें मुझे अच्छी लगती हैं।।
(झूंसी - एक जगह का नाम)

Dr. Pranoti Sakhare

Dr. Pranoti
From the city of Oranges
Dentist by profession
Creative mind
Passionate for writing
Consciousness expressing through Creation
Inspired by Dancing
And Painting is another way to keep my Dairy

Confessions

Deep down the streak
I found some misconception
I tried finding out away
But was not able to play
It all started with the connection
I was not happy with the intention
I was neither been loved
Nor I was treated as an exception
It was an assignment that kept me delaying
Empty was my hand and I kept on waiting
Nothing was I able to do
Nothing was I able to determine
The hatred enhanced day by day
& decreased all my delight
No questions were answered
No solutions were conveyed
I was just kept alive
For the sake of break
It all depended on me
It all depended on the momentum
But I was not ready to walkout
It was my diligence
How do I break down in seconds
How do I need to crush at the moment
My kindness was suffering
With no belief in revoking
I had to bow down
I had to make a decision
I need to realize,
That life is always persistent
It was all mine
As I was just 29

The chapter I had to close
I had no choice
I had to build a new life
It was just the beginning
I had to conquer the world
No one was awaiting
Be happy with what is happening
My heart whispered
It's all for you
And you have to get through
No deed is enduring
No pain is continuing
It will all fade off
Keep the hope prevailing

Ankita Kumari

I am Ankita Kumari, I am basically from Bihar Bhagalpur, I study in Aditi Mahavidyalaya College of Delhi University.

(1)

शांत कराते कराते दुश्मन को,,
हम ही शांत हो चले,,
हम अच्छे बनते बनते शहीद हो चले,,
और ये आतंकी हमारी अच्छाई से हर पल खेल रहे।।
लड़ते हैं जमीन के लिए,,
जो हर जगह है एक ही,,
कश्मीर भी उसी जमीन पर है,,
अब जहां रहते हैं सिर्फ आतंकी ही,,
उठाते हैं हम पर पत्थर वो और कहते हैं,,
हम कुछ करते ही नहीं।।
मरते हैं जब हम पर रोते हैं सभी,,
एहसास तभी होता है मेरे होने का सबको
जब हम शहीद हो जाते हैं और कहते हैं,,
दो लफ्ज़ मेरे बहादुरी वो नेताजी..!!
पर गालिब दर्द तो बहुत होता है,,
अपनों से जुदा होकर.!!
पर एक सुकून लिए है दिल में हम अमर हुए मरे नहीं.!!

2

दायरे में रहो अंकिता।
करेगी अगर,अपनी मन-मानी।
तो हाथ पैर तोड़ देंगे हम तुम्हारी।।
यह वह देश नहीं।
जहां चलती है बेटियों की।।
यह वह देश है,,
जहां चलती है सिर्फ बेटों की।
दायरे में रहो अंकिता।।
घर से निकलती हो।
तो दुपट्टा लिए निकला करो।।
क्योंकि बुरी निगाहें होती है।
तुमपे लोगों की।
दायरे में रहो अंकिता।।
पूछते हैं हम इस समाज के लोगों से।
दायरे में रहना सिर्फ बेटियों को ही क्यों सिखाया जाता है।।
दायरे हैं, तो बेटों को भी दायरे में रहना सिखाओ।
बेटियां तो रहती है दायरे में ही।।
पर तुम्हारा बेटा नहीं रहता है दायरे में मां।
जरा उसे भी सिखाओ दायरे में रहना।।
क्या गलती थी उस बच्ची की।
जो महज थी 6 वर्ष की।।
उसने कौन से दायरे तोड़े थे।
जो उसे भी नहीं छोड़ा, तुम्हारे दरिंदे बेटे ने।।
बेटियों को कैद रखती हो।
करना है कैद,तो बेटा को कैद करो पिंजरे में।
कम-से-कम तुम्हारी बेटियां तो सुरक्षित रहेंगी।।

Jaz Gill

Jaz Gill was born in India and immigrated to Canada at the age of five. Jaz is a poet and lyricist collaborating with artists and singers to create poetry and music. Jaz's passion is to help others heal with the written word.

A Story

It is a Story
One of an uprising within
A war inside
Of a battlefield of broken hearts
And in these palms
A promise
In these eyes
A broken promise
It is a Story of laughter
An echo heard through
The passage of time
Oh there was a time
Innocence was all there was
But in just one moment
The slightest of moments
All Innocence was lost
It is a Story
Of Love...pure and true
Of torment...through and through
From the darkness
daylight will emerge
And from the defeat
Victory shall grow
It is a Story
Of passion that boldly burns
And purpose that turns
The mundane to miraculous
In a soul that yearns and yearns
For its turn
To Shine
Bright...brighter than even the stars
Deeper than all the scars

A Story of an uprising of
The spirit within
Of every loss
And every win

Imroz Raza

He is Imroz from Delhi he is BUMS student from sanskriti unani medical college and hospital
His hobby is afsana nigari and shayri his first book is chemera : an illusion he work as a co writer in many anthologies like sapno ki udaan, la,memorie, tasweer the image of dream love and many more
For more details you can visit his Instagram: -@itz_imz email: - imz43khan@gmail.com

एक अफ़साना

ख्वाबों की उँगली पकड़कर चलना सीख रहा हूँ,
मैं बातों को भूलना सीख रहा हूँ,
तुम्हारी जिंदगी मैं दोस्ती एक पन्ना होगा,
मैं तो उसमे किताब लिखना सीख रहा हूँ,
चार पल और चार अल्फाजों मैं तुम दोस्ती को बयां कर रहे हो,
मैं उसपे अफ़साना लिखना सीख रहा हूँ,
ऐ इमरोज कल तुम्हारा होगा,
इस बात के सहारे जीना सीख रहा हूँ,
तुम्हें मेरे अल्फाज झूठे लगेंगे,
मैं अपनी सच्चाई का सबूत देना सीख रहा हूँ,
ऐ मौत तू क्या सोचता है..!!
मैं तुम्हें चुनौती देना सीख रहा हूँ,
ना कोई मर्ज़ है फिर भी दिल मैं दर्द है,
ऐ दर्द मै तुम्हें झेलना सीख रहा हूँ,
मैं कोई शायर नहीं..।
ना कोई अफ़साना निगार।
फिर भी लिखकर बयां करना सीख रहा हूँ.. ।।

Robin Singh Rathore

This is Robin Singh Rathore ,He is from a Small Village located near Chittorgarh Rajasthan .Currently he is pursuing his B.SC in Agriculture Department from Mewar University, Gangrar. In list of his Hobbies his favourite Hobby is to Write Poems Which came in emergence in Lockdown now He is Giving more attention to it and posted more poems till now on his youtube and Instagram page.

Youtube Channel -Poetry By Robin

Insta Id - @kr_robin_singh_th.putholi

@poetrybyrobi

सुशांत

पटना मे जन्म लिया ;
दिल्ली से वो आया था ।
बिहार का रहने वाला ;
आज सबके दिलों पे छाया था ।
अपनी मेहनत से उसने ;
बड़े मुकाम को पाया था ।
छोटी-सी उम्र मे उसने ;
ऊंचा नाम कमाया था ।
'पवित्र-रिश्ता' मे उसने;
रिश्तों को सुलझाया था ।
दोस्तों के संग रहकर जीना ;
'काई पुछे मे' सिखलाया था ।
संघर्ष भरा ये जीवन अपना ;
'एम.एस.धोनी' मे दिखलाया था ।
'कमो' बनकर उसने;
'छिछोरे ' मे खुब हंसाया था ।
फिर ना जाने किस गम ने ;
उसको इतना सताया था ।
उसका ' दिल बेचारा ;
कुछ बया न कर पाया था ।

Rudra Prasad Das

I am Rudra prasad das from Bhubaneswar, odisha i am a student in Utkal University.

Some Unforgettable Memories-

Before few days ago i had been go to jalandhar, Punjab i was got of you few younger friends, i was very happy and relaxing with them. They were my best friend i love to spend time with them i was excited to play with them and playing time was 7 'o'clock now when i see the clock at 7' o 'pm i remember them near about friends with me, two are girls and five are boys, The two girls are rababneet kaur and vani Agarwal and boys are Kanav goel, harnav singh, gurkaran singh rehal, jihan bassi and sahil sharma for few reasons they were very close to me some of them were-gurkarans birthday , kanav birthday, holi celebrations morning walk and the exciting movement was searching Ghost at haranv's house.

Kanav goel was my best friend when i was there. kanav was a clever guy he was very angry guy but also he was a very kind guy Harnav singh was also one of my best friend he was god in slang language he was shout lot but he was a kind guy , Gurkaran singh rehal was a very clever, discipline guy he was religious and blind believing guy, Jihan bassi was a very helping and cool guy and sahil sharma was a clever and innocent guy, Vani Agrawal was like my sister and she was a very clever and kind hearted , Rababneet kaur was an extraordinary, i treated her like my own sister or you can say more than my sister .she was younger than every children she was very funny and clever just like Tony stark

At last i would like to say that i hope i will meet them again soon i am remembering every movement that i spend with them, may god bless you all

Raman Shant

Raman Shant - I am Raman Shant, belong to Mohali (Punjab). I have been working as UI designer for 6 years. Writing poems and short stories are my hobby and love writing about romance. My motive in life is to touch the soul of people through my writings. Now, I would like to switch my talent into the commercial field so that I could get more reach.
Insta Id - shant_diary

चलो कुछ ऐसा करले......

मोहब्बत तो की थी हमने,
अब वक्त के साथ दर्द को सीने में दफन करले,
चलो कुछ ऐसा करले।

माना कि साथ रहना है अब मुश्किल,
इस मोहब्बत को फासलो में तब्दील करले,
चलो कुछ ऐसा करले।

दूरियां मिटा ना पाएंगी इस दर्द ए गम को, यादों को साथ ले चले,
चलो कुछ ऐसा करले।

सर्द भरी रातों मे जो गुजारे थे हसीन लम्हे,
आखरी दफा फिर से हसीन करले,
चलो कुछ ऐसा करले।

वक्त के साथ यादें धुंधली हो जाएंगी,
इन यादों को पन्नों पे उतारले,
चलो कुछ ऐसा करले।

इस जन्म में हम ना मिले तो क्या हुआ,
खुदा से अगले जन्म की इबादत करले,
चलो कुछ ऐसा करले।

Prayksha Pandit

It's me prayksha Pandit from Nepal and i am studying in 11th standard. I am a law student.
I love vlogging

School Life

I am from middle class family.everyone have some memories in their life whether its good or bad.Bad memories teach a lots of things in our life.whether its bad but we can learn how to stay strong from that memory.I also have experience one of the most worst memory in my life.

Actually, i am thin girl and when i was in class 10 everyone used to bully me. I had few friends only they were good but others used to bully me every time .whenever i tried to say something they used to low my confidence down.They used to teach me .they used to do negative comments on my body.And i tried to scold them but ho could i handle them always? I was average at study but i was discipline student. I was extrovert and friendly but i dont know why they used to teach me laugh at me? whenever we go somewhere i used to be alone no one was with me.I used to cry always at school.Noone was with me.but i never let my confidence down and used to motivate myself Time changes and now i am working in many programs and also i passed SEE and went out from that school.Now maybe they are regreting .So.never feel demotivated .keep loving yourself.

Payal Indani

Co- author Payal Indani is a heartborn girl with lots of love in her eyes.. Heartbroken by her loved one.. Still finds love in everyone.. She is happy with whatever she have and also desires to be a author of her own book very soon.. Love legal practices but firmly interested in reality of everything.. She wants to achieve the nano happiness in life and be a star of her own family like a gem.. She is Co-author in almost a dozen of anthologies and seeks the opportunities in every way she could..

Our Love..

The craziest start of our love.. The desperate ones.. You always wanted to be my side. And I always ran away from you.. Rather from your goggles.. You and your goggles were exact opposite.. You with a soft and sweet heart.. And your goggles were scary as ghost.. But the actual thing which made me fall for you.. Were your eyes.. Heartbroken and beautifully beating for me to be with you forever..
We completed a year together.. But still I feel as if I know you from years.. You gave me the thing which no one ever felt of giving.. People either fall in love or they fail in love.. But when it comes to us.. We neither fall.. Nor fail.. We just love.. Unconditionally.. Truly.. Deeply and madly for each other.. You are that spark in the darkness which gave me a hope to live again.. You are a miracle and true blessing in my life..

Dr Shreeja Singh Chandel

'अभिव्यक्ति मेरे मन की ' काव्य संग्रह की रचनाकार, सताक्षी वूमेन अवार्ड विजेता डॉ० श्रीजा सिंह चंदेल उत्तराखंड की राजधानी देहरादून में एक चिकित्सक हैं, साथ ही भरतनाट्यम व कथक नृत्य में पारंगत हैं। ये बालपन से ही लिखती रही हैं तथा अपने लेखन के द्वारा जीवन के सभी पहलुओं पर अपनी भावाव्यक्ति से मानव जीवन में व्याप्त वेदना, पीड़ा और मानसिक तनाव के पीड़ा बोध को नूतन वेदना दर्शन दे रही हैं।

समर वैकेशन का होमवर्क !

गर्मी की छुट्टियों की शुरुवात थी।

लगता था खुशियों की बारात थी।

मेरी खुशी का कोई ठिकाना न था।

अब रोज स्कूल जाना न था।

ये करूं, वो करूं, आखिर मैं क्या करूं?

ये खेलूं, वो खाऊं, यहां जाऊं, वहां जाऊं।

अब बस्ते का बोझ नहीं, जल्दी उठना भी रोज नहीं।

मेरी शैतानी देख देख मेरी मम्मी घबराई।

फिर उन्होंने मुझको मेरे गर्मी के होमवर्क की याद दिलाई।

मैं बोला,

मां कुछ दिन तो स्वतंत्र रहने दो।

होमवर्क जो जाएगा अभी आराम भी करने दो,।

मेरी मम्मी हैं भोली, इस पर वे कुछ न बोलीं।

मैं था मस्ती में डूबा, दुनिया को पीछे भुला।

जब अंतिम हफ्ता आया तो मेरा दिल घबराया।

खोला देखा जब होमवर्क, दुनिया लगने लगी नर्क।

फिर याद आया,

आज करे सो कल कर, कल करे सो परसों,

इतनी जल्दी क्या है, जब जीना है बरसों।

सोचकर यह बात, अभी तो बचे हैं दिन सात

थोड़ा और आराम कर लूं,

ग्रहण से पहले खुशियां भर लूं

फिर पांच दिन बाद, मुझे होमवर्क की आई याद

होमवर्क का ढेर था, मेरे दिल में अंधेर था।

डर था छूटे ना अधूरा, किसी तरह कर तो लिया पूरा।

स्कूल में इसका इनाम मिला , कि फिर से वो सारा काम मिला।

सब गड़बड़ मैं कर आया था, हर विषय में जीरो पाया था

अब आज मैं फिर पछताता हूं, तुमको भी यह बतलाता हूं।

मुझको आलस्य ने घेरा था।
मन में शैतान का डेरा था।
तुम भी ऐसा कुछ मत करना,
हर काम समय पर ही करना।
कल कल करते, काम से बचते, कल आज में तुम यूं न उलझना।

Pooja Indani

Co-author Pooja Indani is a happy go lucky girl and an extremely extrovert person. She is co-author of more than 20 anthologies. She has done her master's in commerce and aspire to complete her doctorate and add prefix Dr. To her name. She is an hard core painter and an all time teacher. And her slogan for life is Go with the flow. Writing is not just her hobby but she writes her heart out in her every write up.

Life Is Unpredictable.

Me and my partner were having a good bond and we wanted to take this to the next level and wanted to tie into a relationship forever. But it is life, everything doesn't go according to your planning. When we were about to talk to our parents and make the bond permanent. We got to know that he have a clot in right side of his neck and as per the doctor's advice we went for a biopsy. And thought that it's the end but when we got the reports we were shaken and the most unexpected thing happened.

It was not a regular clot it was a clot of cancer. And both of us went into trauma. But some how we both held hand and his treatment started and after long 10 months and 12 chemos his reports were negative.

Everything started to become normal and we were normalising things and 6 months passed by like this.

One day suddenly he started coughing and again we went for certain test and the situation was worsen when we heard the word "Relapse" so now hoping for everything to be fine and getting back to our normal life.

Shweta Taikar

Shweta Taikar, the Marathi girl from Gondia Maharashtra...Loved to express her thoughts in the form of poetry, shayaries, stories, blank verses (most)...on her youtube channel "Eternal Art" where she shares her 10 years of her writting collection over her and other life experiences and places. She has done Masters in Microbiology.. And was working in a Private sector. But for now she is following her intution as she is much intrested in writting. As from childhood to the growing phase of life she found her kin intrest in Litreature.... Writting is something which add emotions to her life...

"कहानी जिससे मैं लेखिका बनी...."

आज मुस्कुरा रही हूं पर,
मुस्कुराने की वजह नहीं जानती ।
आज गुनगुना रही हुँ कुछ, पर सुर नहीं जानती ।
कई दफा लिखने की कोशिश की मैंने,
पर लिखूंगी क्या ये नहीं जानती।
मान बैठी थी मैं कि..
फिर उदासी से घिरा पाऊंगी खुद को,
शायद लिखूंगी कुछ तो...
पर आज जब लिखने की ठानी तो,
अलग ही सुकून मिल रहा है...
लेखिका सुनना लेखिका सुनने में..
कुछ अलग ही मजा आ रहा है ।
कोशिश करती थी की,
अपने मन के हर जज्बात को दबादु ।
उन्हें आवाज तो दिल देता था मेरा पर,
उन्हें हाथों का सहारा देना मुझे मंजूर ना था ।

आज उसी कलम के सहारे मेरा दिल लिख रहा है.....
आज आवाज में कुछ अलग ही खामोशी है ।
यह अखबार में छपते इश्तेहार नौकरी के,
पढ़ती थी और अलग कर देती थी ।
जानती थी कि कुछ नया करूंगी ।
जीवन में वह नयापन ये आज था...
नहीं थी जानती ।
आज खामोश है जुबान तो,
हाथ लिख रहे हैं...
ये जज्बात है मेरे...
ये सलाम लिख रहे हैं....।

आज यकीन आया खुदा की इस मेहरबानी पर...।
कि क्यों चुना उसने मेरे लिए मुझे हर परेशानी पर ।
कि क्यों मैंने कभी उसे कोसा नहीं मुश्किलों में...।
कि तोहफा दिया उसने मुझे आज इस जुबानी में...।
अक्सर सोचती थी मैं की,
कैसे अदा कर पाऊंगी खुदा को,
उसकी मेहरबानी मुझ पर ।
जब देखती थी मैं इन कागजों में...
अपने जज्बातों कि, की नकाशी ।
आज यकीन आता है ।
कि खुद ही अनजान थी,
अपने ही तारूफ से...
नवाजा है खुदा ने जब हमें इस दौलत से ।
महसूस करती हूं खुद को और पाती हूं खुशनसीब ।
जब कबूल की खुदा की रेहमत हमने इस खूबसूरत अंदाज में ।
यही शायद कहानी है मेरे होने की...
कहानी, जिससे मैं लेखिका बनी....।

Ketan Nag (Neeket)

Ketan Nag (Neeket) is a 30 years old boy from U.P. He is a B.Tech Engineer and loves to write as he found it the best way to express his feelings. He aspires to become great poet because of his passion for writing. He wishes to make his parents and friends proud.

"किस्सा बचपन का"

गर्मी की दोपहर में हम सभी लेटे हुए थे कि बाहर आइसक्रीम वाले की आवाज आई "आइसक्रीम,आइसक्रीम"। घर के सभी बच्चे आइसक्रीम लेने के लिए दौड़े। मैं भी अपनी भतीजीयों को लेकर बाहर गया और आइसक्रीम दिलायी। देखा तो बाहर मोहल्ले के लगभग सारे बच्चे इकट्ठा हो चुके थे, सभी अपनी पसंदीदा आइसक्रीम खरीदने में लगे थे। कुछ बड़े लोग भी वहां मौजूद थे मैंने देखा कि एक बच्चा रुपए नहीं लाया था और उसने आइसक्रीम लेने के लिए अपना हाथ बढ़ा दिया पर उस बच्चे के चचेरे भाई ने उसे यह कहकर आइसक्रीम ले ली कि वह उसके लिए नहीं है बल्कि उसकी बहन के लिए है और अगर तुम्हें खाना है तो पैसे लेकर आओ मेरे पापा क्यों दिलाएंगे? यह देख कर मुझे ऐसा लगा मानो मेरा बचपन मेरी आंखों के आगे तैर गया हो।

ठीक से याद तो नहीं पर शायद 18-20 साल पुरानी बात ही होगी। गर्मी की छुट्टियों में मेरी बुआ और उनके बच्चे आए थे। दिनभर खेलकूद में वक्त कब निकल जाता था पता ही नहीं चलता था। मेरे चचेरे भाई-बहन, मैं और बुआ के बच्चे हम सब मजे करते थे। एक दोपहर हम सब बाहर खेल रहे थे कि तभी आइसक्रीम वाला आया। बड़े पापा वहीं थे तो उन्होंने उस आइसक्रीम वाले को बुलाया और सबको आइसक्रीम देने को कहा। सबको ऑरेंज बार मिल रही थी मैंने भी हाथ बढ़ाया कि तभी दीदी ने हाथ से आइसक्रीम लेते हुए कहा कि यह तुम्हारे लिए नहीं बल्कि बुआ के बेटे के लिए है। मुझे अच्छा नहीं लगा पर मैंने कुछ नहीं कहा मेरा मेरे बड़े पापा यह सब देख रहे थे पर उनके मुंह से एक शब्द ना निकला। तभी मम्मी ने आकर मुझे आवाज दी और कहा कि रुपए लेकर आइसक्रीम ले लो। मैं रुपए लेकर जब तक गया वह आइसक्रीम वाला जा चुका था पर उसके जाने का मुझे इतना दुख नहीं था, मुझे दुख तो उस व्यवहार पर था जो मेरे साथ किया गया था। मैं आंखों में पानी लिए सभी को आइसक्रीम खाते देखता रहा। सभी का शोरगुल देखता रहा किसी ने आवाज दी, ख्याल

टूटा तो मेरी भतीजियां मुझे अंदर चलने को कह रही थी पर मेरी नजर तो उस बच्चे पर थी। मैंने देरी ना करते हुए आइसक्रीम वाले को उस बच्चे को आइसक्रीम देने को बोला क्योंकि मैं नहीं चाहता था कि फिर आज एक बच्चा बुरे व्यवहार के चलते आंखों में नमी लेकर घर जाए। इसी एहसास के साथ मैं उस बच्चे की खुशी को आइसक्रीम के साथ टपकते हुए देखता रहा और एक सुखद एहसास अपने दिल में लेकर घर की ओर रवाना हो गया।

Atyam Pujitha

Hi, Pujitha here.
A simple and fun loving girl who love to give voice to my thoughts through my writings.

And I Found Him.

I had never expected that I could find my 'oppa' of my dreams. Don't you know what is oppa? Then I have to travel to 2016 because that is when it all started.

It was one of the rainy and lazy day when I was rolling on my bed. My roommate rushed into our room with her friend's laptop, turned it on and started watching something. I asked her what was she watching so eagerly to which she replied 'korean series.' It was not my first time hearing about them but I never intended to watch. She asked me if I would like to join but I said no. After a while unexpectedly I glanced at the laptop screen while I was drinking water. I never know that fraction of second would make me an addict! It was such a fascinating scene and I fell for male lead on the spot. I pushed my friend aside, rewinded it and started watching the episode.
From then, I especially made my time to watch k-dramas. The way the male leads look after their girlfriends had increased my standards for men. Eventually I started dreaming of my oppa and the qualities he should have. My only wish is that even if my partner doesn't watch k-dramas, at least he should let me watch. My friends used to tease me for my obsession over them.

When my parents started to look for alliance, I even mentioned about my craze in my bio. When I got a request from a guy, he seemed like a fit for all my expectations except for one. On the day of match making when they asked about my hobbies, I said watching K-dramas to which he replied "Even I watch them." Then my heart shouted at me with joy "You found him!"
Yes, I found him, my oppa.

Namita Arora

Namita is a girl from India 18 years of age .She is a budding artist-a writer, a poet and a
Blogger...This personality finds utmost joy in writing about self love. She has been writing since a couple of years...

This Is My Story

The best thing that happened to me and what I endure the most is the time i spent at my school. For me those years were full of amazement, vigour, zest.

In addition to enjoyment, we have learnt a lot of lessons.

Those bountiful years spent are a golden memory.

The place I miss the most, which gave me a new hope every day .The aura that enlightened me as soon as I entered the HEAVEN.

The lovely friends we have right now, the blessings of our GOD LIKE TEACHERS, the daily motivation by our Principal have shaped our minds and our lives in an adorable way.....

Each day I was present there was a day lived.

The fulfilling love we got each day was like honey to our soul .Each person there was our family. Our loving juniors and their company was the best thing .Even now wheen they remember us, is a golden moment for us.

I would like to conclude by saying that places change, people change, time changes, but the thing that remains with us, embedded in our hearts are the memories we create......

Those memories are all what we look back to and feel blessed.

I ve heard that we realise the importance of things when we lose them but I have been enduring every moment spent with all the members of my St Joseph's family.

I am thankful to God for bringing such a great blessing in my life and that too very beautifully.

Asrar Ul Hassan

I live in Kashmir and im studying in first year.

The Spicy Truth

Its not about the knowledge you're gaining it's about the situation what you're looking for.

If you can see the actual depth of things you will learn each and everything by itself. Our creator is Allah he is OMNIPOTENT he knows each and everything because he made us.

When you were child your expectations and dreams were too many but slowly slowly you grew up expectations and dreams forget the path its not easy to hold a dream for too long but if you're willing then its like keeping an old note in pocket, the older it gets,the rearer it becomes. You see in life you're using phones and your elder ones don't know how to use it they feel like, a kid is watching everything but can't do anything.

So just think about that thing when you grow up and marry to your love and when you have some babies and after they will grew up they will do something like you will not know they will teach you like now you're teaching you mom and dad so let you teach them not them to teach you. If you're not good in studies it doesn't mean you ain't genius every mind is a creative mind but not everyone is knowing of that thing.

People will never tell you you're good at this thing because they think he knows that. People will push you up but if youself isn't available and willing for that thing its waste of time. Think like an old behave like a kid listen like a kid and behave like a man.

You see in life your life.

Indeed god is Omnipotent he knows everything.

When i was a child my grandfather used to tell me some stories about EVILS' and sort of ELVES we call them (pariyan). Once my grandfather told me a story of seven brothers that story was tremendous no doubt. Do you wanna hear that? Once upon a time somewhere in a small village there were some hand full of people and specially two old man living close to each other one old man has seven sons and second one also have the same.

But one was happy and another one was unhappy.

Happy one told his sons come with me we are going to the Jungle they all seven standed up fastly and didn't asked any questions like why we are going to jungle there was nothing like that they follow the command of there father and moved towards the jungle. And they saw a good place for stay and there father commanded all of them to collect some woods they standed up and running around collecting some woods and there was a big tree and a huge bird was on the tree watching them working hard and following the command of their respective father. Few minutes later the old man saw the bird on the tree and he command his sons go and get this bird for me, those seven brothers didn't think about anything they just started to climb the tree and then the bird started to feel like they will catch me and kill me after, the bird started to speak with that old man and bird was astonished by them and was so impressed from their fidelity towards father.

The birs told that old man please tell them to stop, yes indeed they will catch me let me go i will give you a box of gem and precious gold.

Old man replied where it is?

Bird replies dig a pit around this tree whome im standing at.

They started digging around the tree and found a box of gem and precious gold in it they all were happy.

Before, they were impoverished.

And now they become rich and they left that bird out there and moved towards the village.

And the second unhappy old man saw them and he was astonished about how they become rich in one night he asked him how and when it happens.

The happy old man told him about all the story of jungle.

And after hearing the magnificent story he was astonished and he said him i will do the same as you. The happy old man replied and said ok that's fine.

Unhappy old man command his children, come with me we are going to the jungle, his children replies and said but why? What is our work in jungle..

He angrily replies and said get up i said get up...
Those sever children stands up disinterestedly
And started following their father.
And they reached at the same place were that happy old man was.. And this one also started to command his children but they were refusing by telling that we don't have energy and wait some time bla bla and that bird on the tree, was watching everything the old man was angry too but his children was refusing again and again.. And after some how they disinterestedly done some kinda work and that bird on the tree was watching everything. After some time the old man commanded all of his children to catch the bird on the tree like same as that happy old man did.
They were like why? How? No no we don't know how to catch bla bla and that bird was laughing on them and said.
Hay dumb people you know it's impossible to catch me but those who came here before you they were following all of their father's commands and i was astonished and i got scared when he commanded for me.
That's why i gived them a treasure.
Stop thinking.start doing.If you think that thinking is better then doing, then you're wrong;as doer is better then sitter.Giving is better than taking.
It's not true, what we are seeing is actually true.
The water is colour less. Okay! Who told you this? Your teacher. Right!
If you yourself become the drop of water or the shower of water then you're able to see everything.If you're the water, you can take any place and form to fulfill it. Don't change yourself to fulfill your joys change them to fulfill both.

Ashita Sharma

Ashita Sharma is a Post graduate in Microbiology from Nagpur whose mind resides in laboratory but her heart lives in writing. She believes in writing with her heart and is a passionate storywriter on wattpad. An ardent poetry lover, she has won many poetry contests and have been a part of more than 50 Anthologies out of which 6 are published and released online. Currently she is compiling three books and is working with NaviEncre Publications. Recently, she has been awarded with the Opus Talent Awards from the team Opus Coliseum. She still looks forward to achieve more in this world of words, aiming to publish her solo book very soon.

The Joy Of Giving

It was in the year 2019 when I visited my cousin at Wardha to celebrate the festival of Rakshabandhan with him. Those were the days when I felt happy, pampered, free and loved. Being the youngest member of my house and not to forget, the only girl child, I have been blessed with the best family one could ever ask for. Since the days of my childhood till turning into an adult, there is nothing I actually lacked. Whatever I wished for was given to me, my demands were fulfilled, my cupboard is always full and I loved materialistic things whether it's a pencil or my notebook or a pen or my set of dolls and teddy bears. These things always made me happy. I believed that to keep myself joyful, these things are needed but one day, my point of view changed, just a small incident happened but it something I will remember for the rest of my life. So yes, coming back to my trip to Wardha, the perception changing incident took place there in that town.

One fine afternoon, me, my aunt and my brother went to a restaurant and had our lunch. The tasty food filled our hearts and stomach. It was time to go back home. But as we had only one vehicle, my brother decided to drop my aunt first. I stayed back and played a few games in the funzone of that place. My eyes shifted to the delicious pastries and so I decided to buy myself one. As it was my brother's treat, I hardly carried money with me but yeah had some to buy atleast one sweet treat for myself. I was about to order when something distracted me. The scene looked pathetic when my eyes witnessed how the owner of the restaurant was treating that little child, a beggar I suppose. He was just asking for something to eat and all he got was this mistreatment. My blood boiled on seeing the owner and my eyes turned watery on noticing the tear striken face of that little boy. He started leaving and that's when I rushed to him. I immediately asked him to stop and he smiled. He by actions told me that he is hungry. I immediately took him inside, much to the owner's surprise.

I asked the little boy his choice and he immediately chose the black forest pastry. I handed him the box and noticed his expression. His face depicted sheer happiness. His face was telling how happy he was at the moment. The little box was not less than any treasure to him and thats when my heart melted, thats when I realised that in life sometimes, happiness is not in what we get but in what we give to others. The little boy smiled and tightly grabbed that box. He then left the place and my brother came to pick me up after a minute. On my way back to home, my eyes didnt leave that little child who was dancing and running with the box in his hand. My smile didnt leave my face and even today when I see a black forest pastry all I could remember is that little boy and the box which was his priceless possession and also the box that gave me a joy of lifetime.

Susmita Kar

Nineteen years old conquering her weakness

What Story A Nineteen Year Old Will Say?

I dont have friends who text me daily. And I really feel lonely about this. It's just me and my books. It wasn't this 5 years ago. I was completely an extrovert having tonnes of good friends who will text me and I text them back. We even meet each other and did innumerable conference calls. I crave for those laughs and giggles. I really miss them. But then I met someone who manipulated me and made me introvert. Obviously I became because I dont like hurting. I know how it feels. This person took me and my feelings granted for like everyday. I am unable to let go of that person because I am attached with love and I dont want to hurt or make that person go through the same pain that I have been inside of me. It really sucks.

I am taken for granted, everytime I speak truth, everytime i explain my self. It is always termed as an excuse. If I say the above all to that person then it would be called ' you are creating drama '. Sometimes I go into deep thinking and start crying again and again, saying myself why it is always me. I am enrolled to a college now, it's been 2months and I haven't made friends. No one texts me. If I keep my data off for like 2-3 days straight away. Nothing changes because i come back online to zero notifications. I want to change things in my life but this pandemic is ruining my ability to cope up. I dont know what should I do. I am so damn broken, that i participate in anthologies to keep me busy and I live writing. I know I am strong enough I will conquer all my weakness and I will succeed. I am enough optimist in my life that I will get ready to keep my life going ahead. Failures aren't draw backs they are your real steps to the stair heading to success. "Fail, fail, fail again and rise like a phoenix " this empowers me to win. And I will definitely succeed.

Flairs and Glairs, a platform by a student for the students. We are esteemed youth struggling to carve out our path for our future and we follow a basic mindset Since everyone is not born with all-round skills. Joining hands with people who are born to execute it with perfection is the best way to evolve. Self-Evolution is the need of the hour but, evolving as a community is what we strive for. The initiative as kickstarted by, Founder- Mr. Shubham Shah with the motive to utilize the skillset and talent of writing has now a team of 10+ people who are actively participating into newer forms of learning and discovering talents among youngsters. We Provide platform and services like Publishing opportunities, Open mics, Workshops, Hands-on training. Operating with Brand Name of Flairs and Glairs (Publication House), we offer the chance of elevating a passionate writer to an esteemed author With Brand name Teekhe Zasbaaat. We bring to you an opportunity to get accustomed with the Public Speaking and Presenting of Thoughts along with regular challenges to brush up your inking spirit. The newest initiative to extend our services we introduced in a new writing Platform- The Glittering Fables and Ink Over Tears.

We Choose to Fly Like A Falcon than to be

a Leg Pulling Crab.

To Know More: Infoline – 7781900870
Mail Us At-
flairsandglairs@gmail.com / info@flairsandglairs.in
Or Visit is at
www.flairsandglairs.com / www.flairsandglairs.in
Social Handles- @flairsandglairs @teekhezasbaaat